Family Violence

Other Books in the Social Issues Firsthand series:

Family Violence

Linda Richards, Book Editor

GREENHAVEN PRESS

An imprint of Thomson Gale, a part of The Thomson Corporation

Detroit • New York • San Francisco • New Haven, Conn. • Waterville, Maine • London

Christine Nasso, *Publisher*
Elizabeth Des Chenes, *Managing Editor*

© 2007 Thomson Gale, a part of The Thomson Corporation.

Thomson and Star logo are trademarks and Gale and Greenhaven Press are registered trademarks used herein under license.

For more information, contact:
Greenhaven Press
27500 Drake Rd.
Farmington Hills, MI 48331-3535
Or you can visit our Internet site at http://www.gale.com

Articles in Greenhaven Press anthologies are often edited for length to meet page requirements. In addition, original titles of these works are changed to clearly present the main thesis and to explicitly indicate the author's opinion. Every effort is made to ensure that Greenhaven Press accurately reflects the original intent of the authors. Every effort has been made to trace the owners of copyrighted material.

Cover photograph reproduced by permission of Roy Morsch/CORBIS.

ISBN-13: 978-0-7377-2887-3
ISBN-10: 0-7377-2887-6

Library of Congress Control Number: 2006936798

Printed in the United States of America
10 9 8 7 6 5 4 3 2 1

Contents

Chapter 2: Family Violence Affects Others Outside of the Family

Chapter 3: Ending the Violence

Foreword

Social issues are often viewed in abstract terms. Pressing challenges such as poverty, homelessness, and addiction are viewed as problems to be defined and solved. Politicians, social scientists, and other experts engage in debates about the extent of the problems, their causes, and how best to remedy them. Often overlooked in these discussions is the human dimension of the issue. Behind every policy debate over poverty, homelessness, and substance abuse, for example, are real people struggling to make ends meet, to survive life on the streets, and to overcome addiction to drugs and alcohol. Their stories are ubiquitous and compelling. They are the stories of everyday people—perhaps your own family members or friends—and yet they rarely influence the debates taking place in state capitols, the national Congress, or the courts.

The disparity between the public debate and private experience of social issues is well illustrated by looking at the topic of poverty. Each year the U.S. Census Bureau establishes a poverty threshold. A household with an income below the threshold is defined as poor, while a household with an income above the threshold is considered able to live on a basic subsistence level. For example, in 2003 a family of two was considered poor if its income was less than $12,015; a family of four was defined as poor if its income was less than $18,810. Based on this system, the bureau estimates that 35.9 million Americans (12.5 percent of the population) lived below the poverty line in 2003, including 12.9 million children below the age of eighteen.

Commentators disagree about what these statistics mean. Social activists insist that the huge number of officially poor Americans translates into human suffering. Even many families that have incomes above the threshold, they maintain, are likely to be struggling to get by. Other commentators insist that the statistics exaggerate the problem of poverty in the United States. Compared to people in developing countries, they point out, most so-called poor families have a high quality of life. As stated by journalist Fidelis Iyebote, "Cars are owned by 70 percent of 'poor' households. . . . Color televisions belong to 97 percent of the 'poor' [and] videocassette recorders belong to nearly 75 percent. . . . Sixty-four percent have microwave ovens, half own a stereo system, and over a quarter possess an automatic dishwasher."

However, this debate over the poverty threshold and what it means is likely irrelevant to a person living in poverty. Simply put, poor people do not need the government to tell them whether they are poor. They can see it in the stack of bills they cannot pay. They are aware of it when they are forced to choose between paying rent or buying food for their children. They become painfully conscious of it when they lose their homes and are forced to live in their cars or on the streets. Indeed, the written stories of poor people define the meaning of poverty more vividly than a government bureaucracy could ever hope to. Narratives composed by the poor describe losing jobs due to injury or mental illness, depict horrific tales of childhood abuse and spousal violence, recount the loss of friends and family members. They evoke the slipping away of social supports and government assistance, the descent into substance abuse and addiction, the harsh realities of life on the streets. These are the perspectives on poverty that are too often omitted from discussions over the extent of the problem and how to solve it.

Greenhaven Press's Social Issues Firsthand series provides a forum for the often-overlooked human perspectives on society's most divisive topics of debate. Each volume focuses on one social issue and presents a collection of ten to sixteen narratives by those who have had personal involvement with the topic. Extra care has been taken to include a diverse range of perspectives. For example, in the volume on adoption, readers will find the stories of birth parents who have made an adoption plan, adoptive parents, and adoptees themselves. After exposure to these varied points of view, the reader will have a clearer understanding that adoption is an intense, emotional experience full of joyous highs and painful lows for all concerned.

The debate surrounding embryonic stem cell research illustrates the moral and ethical pressure that the public brings to bear on the scientific community. However, while nonexperts often criticize scientists for not considering the potential negative impact of their work, ironically the public's reaction against such discoveries can produce harmful results as well. For example, although the outcry against embryonic stem cell research in the United States has resulted in fewer embryos being destroyed, those with Parkinson's, such as actor Michael J. Fox, have argued that prohibiting the development of new stem cell lines ultimately will prevent a timely cure for the disease that is killing Fox and thousands of others.

Each book in the series contains several features that enhance its usefulness, including an in-depth introduction, an annotated table of contents, bibliographies for further research, a list of organizations to contact, and a thorough index. These elements—combined with the poignant voices of people touched by tragedy and triumph—make the Social Issues Firsthand series a valuable resource for research on today's topics of political discussion.

Introduction

Experts agree that family violence is about power and control. It is a pattern of behavior used by one person in a relationship to exert control over another. Although the terms family violence and domestic violence are used interchangeably, domestic violence usually involves violence between intimate partners, while family violence encompasses more types of abuse, including the maltreatment of children.

Physical abuse—such as hitting, pushing, arm-twisting, or injury with a weapon—is the most frequently reported type of family violence. Other criminal forms of family violence, however, include stalking, sexual abuse, and incest. The term is even broad enough to include emotional abuse, which may take the form of intimidation, continual belittling through insults, threats to kill, the abuse of pets, and economic manipulation such as withholding money from a partner or preventing a partner from obtaining a job.

Family violence, in all its forms, may occur continuously or sporadically. It usually becomes an established cycle, however, with abusive episodes followed by apologies and promises that things will get better. Family violence also commonly follows a pattern of escalation, beginning as verbal abuse or emotional abuse with intent to intimidate and isolate, and then progressing to physical abuse. However, family violence does not have to be physical; verbal abuse alone can be considered family violence.

Adult Victims of Family Violence

According to the Bureau of Justice Statistics, family violence accounted for one in ten cases of reported and unreported violence between 1998 and 2002. Almost half of the episodes were directed against a spouse, and almost three-fourths of the alleged abusers were male. Females are the most likely victims of family violence, with as many as one in three adult women suffering abuse by an intimate partner during her lifetime. This increases to two in every three adult women on welfare. Immigrant women also have higher rates of family violence. This is possibly due to different family dynamics and culturally distinct definitions of abuse, but language barriers, distrust of legal systems, and economic dependency also influence immigrants' decisions not to escape the violence.

Men and gay partners are also victims of family violence. While hospital and police records show relatively few cases of family violence in which men are victimized, those who research male abuse believe the low numbers are due to the fact that men are less likely to seek out services or fear the police will not believe their story. As one man abused by his wife said, "People always looked at me dubiously if I told them that my ex-wife had abused me. I'm much bigger than she was, and I'm sure they find it difficult to understand how that could happen." Such testimony leads some experts to say that the true number of abused men is greatly underreported.

Factors that May Increase the Risk of Family Violence

There is no clear character portrait of a victim or perpetrator of family violence. Researchers are unable to isolate a single trait or risk factor that characterizes a batterer or offending person. This suggests that a complex combination of circumstances and personality traits are responsible in many situations. For instance, alcohol or drug use, which statistics show are involved in about four of ten cases, can increase the frequency of the abuse, but most experts agree that these substances do not cause the abuser to act out. They may, however, impair the judgment of the abuser, allowing him or her to accept and use violence or intimidation as a means of control.

In addition, many people mistakenly assume abuse victims have low self-esteem, or else they would stand up to or escape their tormentors. Although the shame and embarrassment of the abusive relationship may ultimately lower a victim's self-esteem, those victimized by abusive partners choose to stay in these relationships for various reasons. Some, for example, may be living in poverty in which the abuser's income is necessary to run the household.

Family violence, however, is not an income-based or class-based issue. It happens to all types of families. Susan Weitzman, a psychotherapist in Chicago and lecturer at the University of Chicago, found herself confronting this fact when a client—the wealthy, highly educated wife of a prominent sociologist—suddenly confessed that she was a battered woman. Now an author of the book *Not to People like Us*, Weitzman reports that more than 60 percent of the high-income women she has seen in counseling have suffered or are now suffering from spousal abuse. While unemployment, alcohol, and drugs are common factors in lower-income abuse situations, Weitzman says men in upscale abuse situations believe they are above the law, and their rage commonly erupts when their demands are not met.

Violent Children and Victimized Children

Family violence can also involve people of all ages. Elderly parents are sometimes abused in the home by their adult children. Their dependency and inability to fight back often makes them easy targets of verbal and physical abuse. Some younger parents are also victimized by their children's abusive behavior. Although there are few recent statistics, a 1980 study showed that as many as one in three children between the ages of three and seventeen hit their parents each year. Mothers are the likely victims of such attacks. Additionally, findings from the National Family Violence Survey suggest 7 million children in the United States are seriously beaten up by a sibling at least once in their lifetime.

More common, however, are child victims of abusive parents. Indeed, young children are often victims of family violence because they are usually weak and entirely dependent on their abusers. One out of every ten cases of family violence involves a parent physically abusing a child. Surveys also show that men who frequently assault their wives also frequently abuse their children. However, regardless of whether children themselves experience physical abuse, they can still suffer the trauma of growing up in an abusive home. Studies suggest that between 3 and 10 million children witness some form of domestic violence annually. Some of these children mature under a belief that violence is a normal way to express anger and resolve family issues. As grown-ups, they are more likely to repeat the cycle.

Ongoing Hurdles in Ending Family Violence

Breaking away from the cycle of violence is often a long, difficult, and dangerous process. Although abuse victims may periodically escape their tormentors, many return to the abusive relationship because of misplaced loyalty or dependence on the abuser. For example, studies show that half of the women who go to shelters later return to their partners. Other studies indicate the average battered woman leaves her abusive relationship seven times before making a permanent break. Severing the tie, however, does not always mean that the abuse ends. Because abuse is about control, the abusers do not typically accept their victims' right to freedom. Therefore, a victim's risk of serious injury or death drastically increases after leaving an abusive partner. In fact, over half of all victims who are murdered by intimate partners have already left their abusers.

There is also debate over how to respond to the needs of victims of family violence. Since the late 1980s, most viewed domestic violence as a crime perpetrated primarily by men against women, with many laws passed that mandated arrests for domestic assault and encouraged prosecution. For example, the Violence Against Women Act in 1994 institutionalized family violence on a federal level and was based on the assumption that domestic violence involves male power and control over women. Some argue, however, that the dynamic is more complex and that the response to family violence should examine female as well as male patterns of abuse.

Currently, mandatory arrest laws and restraining orders are the primary legal responses to domestic violence. Under arrest laws, when police intervene in a domestic assault, one partner, usually the man, is arrested to put an end immediately to the violent episode. Some criminologists contend, however, that this response does not lead to a reduction in violence and can cause it to escalate when the arrested individual is released. Author and researcher Linda Mill concludes in her 2003 book, *Insult to Injury: Rethinking Our Responses to Intimate Abuse*, that aggressive police and court intervention is not always the route to diminishing violence. She maintains that the lives and attitudes of the family members must also be addressed through counseling if patterns of violence and abuse are to change.

In *Social Issues Firsthand: Family Violence*, a variety of personal narratives illustrate some of the complex issues that surround domestic abuse. The authors' stories reveal that while similarities exist, circumstances, perpetrator behaviors, and victim responses are varied, ensuring that no two tales of family violence are the same. Some of these stories shed light on the struggles faced by abusers as they confront the patterns of abuse in their own lives. Others tell of the unique courage victims need to break free of the violence that cripples their self-worth and destroys the special bonds of family.

CHAPTER 1

Incidents of
Family Violence

My Mother's Death Should Be a Warning to Others

Teresa Lynn Curlin

In the following selection, twenty-seven-year-old Teresa Lynn Curlin tells the story of how her father shot and murdered her mother during a domestic dispute and then turned the gun on himself. Curlin was 17 years old at the time, and she was summoned from a neighboring house by her younger brother and sister, who were present in the family home when the violent incident took place. After moving on to a marriage in which she, too, became a battered wife, Curlin says she is determined to speak about the violence in her life to encourage others to get out of abusive situations before it is too late.

The first shot rang out at 3:30 a.m., August 3, 1985. The one that killed my mother. . .

I came out of a deep sleep already sitting up, with a dark panicked knot in my stomach. Every cell in my body was aware that something bad had happened. My little sister and (soon to be) mother-in-law were coming downstairs to get me. My little sister said, "Dad hurt mom, there's blood all over." I was already in shock.

I grabbed my robe and ran up the street to my parent's house. The door was locked. I ran to the side door, it was locked too. As I stood there, my boyfriend ran up beside me. He turned to me and said, "We have to call the police, there's a bullet hole through the curtain." This is where my memory gets blurred and I start to lose concept of time. I'm not sure I can tell everything that happened at the exact order, or the exact way it happened. I went in to such a deep state of shock that I would walk right into people and not realize they were even there until after the fact.

No Survivors

When I got back down the street to my boyfriend's parents' house, which was three houses down the street from my parents', my boyfriend was on the phone with the police. Several officers arrived at my parents house. The S.W.A.T. team arrived. They jumped from a cube van loading their pump action shotgun as they ran to surround my parents' home. A half circle of S.W.A.T. officers surrounded the side door with guns ready. One of the officers, standing to the side (just like on T.V.), unlocked the door and pushed it open. Five or ten minutes later, the police chaplin came and told us there appeared to be no survivors.

I walked into the house to tell my little brother and sister. I took one look at them and ran to the bathroom. I could not face them. I couldn't tell them. They had lost so much. I don't know who told them.

We all went to the police station to give statements. I don't know how long we were there, it must have been hours. My boyfriend's father, I was told later, had to pull over several times to vomit on the way home. He knew that could have easily been himself and his wife. We had quite a history with guns. He liked to play Russian roulette with her.

When we got back, there were two ambulances waiting to transport my parents' bodies, and a couple of police cars. When the police were done taking video and photographs of the crime scene which was once our family home, the house was released to us. We were told to contact the coroner's office about having someone come to clean it.

What Happened

You see, my little brother and sister were sleeping in the house when my mother was shot. My parents had been separated a couple of months. He had apparently came to pick up some of his things. They must have argued, no one knows. There is no reason or rhyme to this.

The shot woke my little sister. She saw my Dad dragging my Mom down the basement stairs. She said that she would never forget the sound of our Mother's head hitting each step on the way down. My Father told her to get her brother and to go down the street to get me.

While the police were surrounding the house, my Father lay down beside my Mother and shot himself in the head with her .22 caliber handgun. He died instantly. That was approximately 4 a.m.

The coroner told me that my Mother was unconscious from the time she was shot until the time that her physical body died. I wondered then, as I do still, if that was true. It could have been the most comfort the coroner could offer to a destroyed seventeen year old girl.

I Continued the Cycle

I am telling my story in hopes that it will open your eyes and your minds. The domestic violence must stop. Believe it or not, I almost became my Mother's "prodigy." I went on to marry that boyfriend that I wrote about. He would have killed me one horrible night if not for the intervention of a neighbor.

It's horrible to sit terrified and screaming, clutching your terrified and screaming children, knowing that, with one more good kick, that door is coming down, and once it does . . . [you're] dead.

Don't be my mother. Don't be me. If he hits you once, he'll hit you again. Oh, there's always the hearts and flowers stage when he'll come crawling back with gifts and apologies. He says he'll never hurt you again. But . . . he will. And then he will be back with more gifts and apologies. Each time he will hurt you worse. Sometimes, they even threaten to kill themselves. If you leave—guilt trip. My ex-"husband" and I both lived through that little episode. It's pretty common to these relationships also, unfortunately.

Have the Courage to Leave

Gather up every ounce of courage you have, borrow it from your friends if you have to. Leave. Even if you have to plan it out for a time when he's at work or out of the house. That's what I did. Go to a shelter. There are many, many resources there to help and protect you.

I know that you're scared, even terrified. Maybe more of the thought of life on your own than of him. Call the police. I know you're afraid that he'll get out of jail and come after you, more angry than ever. That is what the shelters are for, to hide you and protect you.

Take pictures of all your cuts, bruises and lumps. The more you document, the more firepower you have. The better chance you have of getting him locked away. The better chance he has of getting the help he needs to stop hurting others and himself.

No Alternatives

Don't fool yourself by believing, as I did, that "he just has problems, if I stick by him and love him, and help him through this, all will be wonderful". Or, "He's a good person deep inside, he just needs to be loved and nourished." He may be a good person, but he does have problems and you, I regret to say, just cannot fix them. He, most likely, does need to be loved and nourished, but not at the expense of your life!

If you have children, you have no other alternative but to leave. If you stay, you are teaching your children to be abusers and victims. If you stay and you have children, you are adding more links to the chain of violence through your children. They will grow to abuse their spouses or to find spouses that abuse them, whether it be mental or physical. They themselves will have mental and emotional problems. Be the Mother for your children that you yourself probably never had. Break the chain of violence. You owe it to your children. You brought them into this world, do not pass this legacy on to them. Life was not meant to be lived this way.

All of this I know from experience. I have not gone to college, I have not finished my G.E.D. I don't have a degree hanging on the wall. This has all, at one time, been my reality. I am a survivor!

After my parents died, I thought people would see me as a freak if I told them. Not once have I found that reaction. If anything, it has made people more aware to meet someone that this has actually happened to. Awareness is our salvation.

I even felt guilt. I felt that somehow I had caused this to happen. I have since realized that I cannot be responsible for another persons actions. I did not put the gun in his hand.

The hardest thing I have to deal with is the fact that my Father, my Dad, is a murderer. I idolized him as a child. He was my "Superman". He just could not live with the thought of life without my Mother. I watched him fall apart day by day. He was extremely dependent upon her. I guess you could call it a fatal attraction. He took my Mother away from me and I hate him for it. But, I love him. He was, after all, my Daddy.

A Happy Second Marriage

I am leading a happy life now. I have been remarried for five years. My husband has never raised a hand to me. The pain goes away. Sometimes it comes back when you're thoughtful and full of memories. I have shed tears as I write this. I am finishing on the tenth anniversary of my parents' death, August 3, 1995.

I Was Molested by My Cousin

Erin Merryn, as told to Jessica Blatt

Erin Merryn is the pseudonym of a college student who was molested by her male cousin. The molesting first occurred when she was eleven years old and lasted two years. In the following selection, she tells reporter Jessica Blatt how she initially stayed silent because she was afraid of the repercussions on their close families, and she feared no one would believe her. She then recounts how she came to realize that her cousin had also sexually abused her younger sister. Eventually the sisters told their shocked parents, forever changing the relationships with their cousin's family. Merryn has written the book Stolen Innocence: Triumphing over a Childhood Broken by Abuse: A Memoir. *Jessica Blatt has written numerous articles as a reporter and is now the style editor at* Philadelphia Magazine.

M y dad comes from a family of seven brothers and sisters, and most of them live near us in suburban Chicago. So as a child, I was really close with all of my cousins. One of my dad's sisters had four boys, and two of them— Brian and Mike[1] —were around the same age as my two sisters and me, so we spent lots time with them. They lived just down the block from us, and every day after school, my sisters and I would go over to their house to hang out. I loved being around them—especially Brian. He was almost three years older than me, a superstar football player and the "golden boy" of the family. Since I didn't have any brothers, Brian sort of filled that role. We'd wrestle, build forts—all the stuff you do with a big brother. It was so much fun.

---

1. All names have been changed.

Erin Merryn, as told to Jessica Blatt, "I Was Molested by My Cousin," *Cosmogirl*, November 2005. Reproduced by permission of the author and subject.

A Horrible Dream?

One night in August 1996, when I was 11, I was staying at my grandparents' condo in Wisconsin with my older sister and our cousins. I woke up in the middle of the night to something strange: Brian, then 14, was lying next to me—he had his hand down my pajama pants and underwear, and he was touching my privates. I didn't know anything about sex then, so I had no idea what he was doing—all I knew was that it felt *wrong*. So I pulled his hand away and placed it gently on his chest, thinking he was sleeping. When I looked at him again, his eyes were open—but he quickly closed them. I didn't know what to do, so I just lay awake all night, curled up in a ball, wondering what had just happened. Brian slept beside me all night.

The next morning, I didn't say anything to anyone. Instead, I just told myself it was a nightmare.

Strike Two

I managed to convince myself that the incident never happened and hung out with Brian like normal. But six months later, my cousins and I were playing hide-and-seek, and Brian led me to a crawl space in the basement to hide. I went inside and lay down—and then Brian got in after me. He covered us with a blanket to "hide," then put his hand down my pants. I screamed. "Leave me alone!" and tried to push him away, but he was too strong. He started humping me and moaning— but just then, we heard my aunt coming. Brian ran upstairs, and I straightened my clothes, went upstairs, and left as if nothing was wrong. Again, I was too scared to tell anyone, I thought they either wouldn't believe me or I'd get in trouble for not telling the first time.

Secrets and Lies

Over the next two years Brian kept finding ways to corner me. Mostly he'd touch me "down there," but sometimes he'd try to make me grab his penis—I'd always make a fist to avoid it. While he was molesting me, he'd tell me to be quiet, and he'd pinch me really hard on the butt if I made any noise. I was terrified he was going to rape me someday. By the time I was 13, it was happening a couple of times a week. But I never told anyone because he'd always say, "If you tell, it'll destroy our family. Besides, no one will believe you—you have no proof."

It never occurred to me that Brian was doing this to anyone else. But in March 1998, my sister Allie, who was 11, blurted, "Brian's gross!" Right then I knew: He'd done it to her too. I thought, if I'd spoken up, I could've protected my little sister. But after talking about it, we were relieved—with both of us saying that it happened, people *had* to believe us.

We told our parents everything. They were totally shocked, and my mom felt like a bad mother for not knowing. I hated that she blamed herself—it wasn't her fault. But it felt so good to have gotten this horrible secret out. My dad went to Brian's mother and told her what he'd done, but when she confronted Brian about it, he claimed Allie and I were making it up—and she believed him. My aunt started avoiding our family and tried to turn the rest of our relatives against us. Brian's promise—and my worst fear—had come true. Our family was destroyed. On top of that, I'd started having nightmares about all the stuff Brian had done to me. And I couldn't date because I just didn't trust guys—I mean, if my own *cousin* could do that to me, who else might?

Facing the Enemy

It wasn't until I was 18 that I realized what I needed to do: I *had* to confront Brian. So I typed everything that was in my head into an e-mail: "In dreams, I've thrown you off cliffs, tied you to trees, fed you to the bears, and tied you in a large black garbage bag and watched you suffocate." I didn't expect a response, but I got one. "I know I messed up as a teenager," wrote Brian, then 20. "But God has given me another chance in life and I'm making the best of it." I was annoyed that he was so casual about it and didn't even apologize, so I wrote back asking him why he did certain things, like this one time he molested me in his basement. His response was, "I don't recall that. . . . I never once fondled you there." It made me so angry! I kept writing, trying to get him to take responsibility and show some remorse. Finally, he wrote the words I never thought I'd hear: "I'm sorry for what I did to you. . . . I wish I could go back and stop myself."

Brian's 23 now and in his last year of college. I see him around sometimes when I'm home during the summer, but we don't talk—I still don't trust him. And I just want to move on with my life. I'm in my second year of college, and I speak about my experiences in various cities through the Children's Advocacy Center. I want to give other kids the strength to speak up. People are so embarrassed to talk about sexual abuse—especially if it's a family member who has abused them, because incest is such a taboo topic. They feel dirty admitting that their first sexual experience was with a relative. But the truth is, they have *nothing* to be ashamed of—I want to help them understand that. And it helps me too, because with every step I take forward. I stop looking back at my past.

The Damage of Verbal Abuse

Annie Kaszina

In the following article, Dr. Annie Kaszina tells the story of a young couple, Julie and Scott, whose relationship is marred by Scott's verbal abuse. She then shares the story of her husband's verbally abusive behavior, and how she finally left her marriage after recognizing the resulting damage on both her and their daughter. Kaszina describes verbal abuse as a form of emotional control. She shows through these examples how such abuse can lead to the diminishment of one partner until it can become difficult for that partner to leave the relationship. Kaszina, however, encourages sufferers of verbal abuse to break free of these debilitating relationships before it is too late. Kaszina is an author of The Woman You Want to Be *and a personal coach in London, England, where she helps women rebuild their confidence and their lives after abusive relationships.*

Julie fell in love with Scott at first sight. It happened at the bus stop when she was 16 on her way back from her first day at college. She'd sprained her ankle and a friend was half-supporting, half-carrying her. Despite the pain she couldn't help but notice the good looking guy waiting at the bus stop. Scott looked at her and his first words to her were that she was 'a drunken c**t'. Julie thought that was hilarious.

By the time she got off the bus they had exchanged phone numbers. They started dating and within weeks had decided they were each other's perfect partner. They soon got engaged. The relationship was passionate, tempestuous with tremendous highs and lows.

Five years later, Julia and Scott are still together and Julie's confidence is shot to pieces. Scott still tells her he loves her,

Annie Kaszina, "The Truth about Verbal Abuse," www.joyfulcoaching.com, 2006. Reproduced by permission.

from time to time, but spends a lot more time telling her how stupid, lazy, ugly and fat she is. And, of course, how lucky she is to have someone like him, because nobody else would want her. The sad thing is, she believes him totally. She's been so brainwashed by him for so long.

Words Can Hurt

We live in a society where people habitually say rude, abrasive, sometimes clever, things to each other, which *are* often quite funny. But rude, abrasive words have the power to chip away at a person until they break them into small pieces.

And we live in a society where we aren't very good at seeing the big picture: if words make us laugh, then they can't be damaging. Domestic violence is a situation in which one person, still statistically more likely to be the man, strikes their partner and/or the children. If there are no physical blows then it can't be violence, can it?

Actually, it can. Domestic violence is a term that describes any situation where one person deliberately, and consistently, hurts another.

Verbal abuse is, correctly speaking, verbal violence. The old adage says: "Sticks and stones will break my bones, but words can never hurt me." It's an utter nonsense. Words, if spoken by someone whose opinion of you, you care about, can shatter you into a thousand pieces.

Had [Nazi German leader Adolf] Hitler not been able to use words so effectively in the first place he would never have won support and never have come to power. Hitler was a past-master of verbal violence. Did his verbal violence pave the way for physical violence, or simply go hand in hand with physical violence? It hardly matters here. What does matter is to be aware that the destructive power of verbal violence is huge. Whether or not, as often happens in time, verbal violence escalates into physical violence.

Emotional abuse, correctly speaking, is emotional violence; as anyone who has ever experienced it will know. The difference between verbal and emotional abuse or violence is illusory. Maybe verbal abuse *sounds* less destructive, but it works through emotional brainwashing and brutality. Telling someone who loves you that they disgust you, repeatedly, will devastate them psychologically.

Mental abuse, correctly speaking, is mental violence. All verbal, emotional and physical violence is mental abuse. Mental abuse occurs whenever one person in a relationship attempts to gain unconditional power and control over the other person.

When it is done through physical intimidation it's easy enough to spot; although women will still, frequently, make excuses like: "He was drunk", "He's had a hard time" etc. Mental abuse is designed to smash another person's self-confidence so that they become emotionally dependent; which then becomes another 'fault' they can be criticized for.

My Story

Like Julie, I spent years in a verbally abusive relationship; in my case, a marriage. My then husband had had a difficult childhood. He was sensitive, vulnerable, and he also had a touch of the 'bad boy' about him. It was an intoxicating mixture. I felt that I could care for him and make him happy. I was also flattered by the way he became so passionate about me so fast.

I didn't know that fast wooing is a key sign of an abuser. They come into a relationship hungry for the status, the sense of well being and power that they get from having someone fall deeply in love with them. They woo fast, because they need to hook their partner in before he/she really starts to see their dark side. They woo fast because while they can come out with all the right words, and acts, and maybe even mean them at the time, it's not love that really drives them, but having their needs met. They get their needs met by draining the life, the spirit, the independence, the joy, out of their partner. They are emotional vampires.

Our courtship was brief. I didn't know it at the time but each time I committed a little more of myself to him he started to behave worse. There was the first time that he screamed: "What the hell do you expect from me" for no apparent reason. After half an hour he was fine. On our honeymoon he refused to speak to me for 24 hours. Then he was as loving as before. The fights and the silences became more frequent and longer.

I didn't get it at all. I didn't realise that he was throwing temper tantrums and sulking and then starting the whole cycle all over again. At first when he was nice, I'd ask him why he'd said all those mean things, and he'd say he didn't mean them. In time, he stopped being nice and I stopped asking.

But he still told me, occasionally, that he loved me, and I was more desperate than ever to believe him. Partly because he didn't like them, partly because I was ashamed to admit what was happening, I stopped seeing my friends and family. The more isolated I became, the more dependent I became on him. And the more careless and cruel he was in his treatment of me.

In public, of course, we acted like there wasn't a problem. I could almost convince myself there wasn't a problem: *he loved me, didn't he?* And I loved him. I thought he had so much potential to become the man of my dreams (*despite all the evidence to the contrary*). Our friends thought we had the perfect marriage; they thought he was as caring and sensitive as he appeared to be in public. He told everyone he was a nice guy, and they believed him.

Breaking Free

It took me over 20 years to realise the damage that had happened to me and to our child, who saw—and understand—

the stark reality long before I did. Then it took a while to start unpicking the web of lies he'd spun around me.

Actually, other people did like and value me. Other men did find me attractive. There were a lot of men out there who were an awful lot nicer, and kinder, than he ever was. I had all sorts of skills, talents and qualities that he had never recognised, never nurtured. The world was not the cruel, destructive place that he had said; that was *his* dark reality that he had visited on me. It didn't have to be mine.

Recently I was talking, socially, to a wonderful lady in her seventies about a domestic violence poster for our local refuge. She said that people don't understand that verbal abuse can be just as damaging as physical violence. She'd been married to a verbally abusive man for 50 years; because her generation stayed married. But she'd suffered terribly, not least because he always presented himself to the world as a delightful gentle man. The years of her widowhood had been the happiest and freest of her life.

Nobody should lose years, or even months, of their life in the misery, humiliation and fear of an abusive relationship. If anyone says mean things about you and won't stop when you tell them not to, because it's upsetting you, that is abusive. That person is giving you a clear sign that they don't care about your feelings—no matter what excuse they make later. If they don't care about your feelings, make no mistake, they will smash into you whenever they want to, just to make themselves feel better. That is the reality of a verbally abusive relationship.

The abuser acts as if he/she has a license to hurt the other person. Each time you accept it and give him/her, or the relationship, another chance, you are endorsing his/her right to hurt you. You cannot help another person to change. You cannot change them by offering them the love they never had. You can only tear yourself into bite sized chunks of raw flesh that they will devour whenever they feel hungry. That is exactly what you can expect.

If you are prepared to end up as a whitening pile of bones at the end of the relationship, while your partner moves on to feed on fresh prey, then go for it. If not, then I suggest you listen very carefully, right from the start, to the words they say. If, ever, they are dismissive of you, or even if they put you on a pedestal but are dismissive of other people, then run. It won't be too long before they turn their savagery on you. A pedestal is no protection at all. Protestations of love are no protection at all. Predators feed on raw meat and abusers *are* predators, whether the violence they use is verbal, emotional, mental or physical.

Suffering through a Violent and Controlling Relationship

David

In the following narrative, a gay man known only as David, tells how he overlooked his boyfriend's controlling behavior when they first met. The physical violence didn't begin until the couple moved together to a different city where David had no friends. David withdrew socially and felt his identity slip away as he struggled with his boyfriend's claim that violence was a part of his culture, and that it was David that needed to change. Only after a friend sent David a book containing a checklist on abusive relationship behavior did David face reality. The author is a resident of Australia who is in his late twenties.

I met Anthony through work when I was 22. The relationship seemed ok in the beginning, but in hindsight, there were warning signs of what was to come. They were little things at first: coming over unannounced; showing up unexpectedly when I was out with my friends; phone calls that seemed to be a little too frequent. I made the mistake of interpreting these early signs as strong romantic interest. Before long he had moved in with me and his behaviour had become obsessive and controlling.

Anthony was really threatened by my friends and my social life. He hated that other guys would look at me, or that I'd slept with other guys around our neighbourhood, even that I had quite a lot of friends who he felt "competed" with him. Tiny things that had not even occurred to me as being possibly offensive would cause enormous rage. The more I was attacked, the more and more I withdrew. It was a self-defence mechanism—I figured if I could stay away from any-

David, "Terrified to Go Home," *AIDS Council of New South Wales*, February 2005. Reproduced by permission.

thing that might cause him to get upset then that would keep him calm. That didn't work of course—he simply found new things to be insecure about. I realise now the whole strategy was to keep me feeling perpetually blamed, inadequate and not doing enough to keep the relationship together. I isolated myself from my friends, my family and from everything that I used to enjoy doing. To get me away from my previous life, friends and sex partners we moved to a different city where I knew no one except him.

I was by nature a very happy, outgoing person, but I quickly became cautious and scared all the time. My fear escalated when the physical violence began. The first time was because he had seen me talking to someone I'd had a fling with in the past and he punched me in the face because of it. From that time on, even though the physical violence was occasional, the fear of it happening pervaded my life and he would threaten me with it often. Punching, pushing, restricting my physical movements (like blocking doors if I was trying to leave a heated situation), destroying or giving away my property and refusing to take care of me if I was sick were punishments that would be meted out when simply threatening me or humiliating me in public wasn't enough.

Using Culture as an Excuse for Violence

Anthony was from a racial minority. One of the biggest headf***s was being told that the violence was part of his "culture" and the fact that I had a problem with it meant that I was racist. The problem according to him was not the violence—it was the fact that my racism meant I couldn't accept who he was. It was me not him, that had to change. I now understand that violence is not culture—there is no ethnic group on the planet that celebrates partner abuse as a cultural identity.

Apart from my massive social withdrawal, the affect on my sexuality was really destructive. I became ashamed about being gay, about being sexually attractive and about having sexual desires. It was like going back in the closet.

Money was another big problem. Successive rent periods came where Anthony would spend all of his pay on gambling and alcohol within 48 hours of receiving it, leaving me to pay all the rent and then provide food for us for a fortnight—impossible and it meant instant poverty. As a "solution", Anthony put me in control of his finances but it was only a licence for him to be as irresponsible as he liked and simply demand more money whenever he wanted it. Of course, refusing because the rent needed to be paid for example, was a dangerous move. On top of all of this, he would also frequently get me to do his work for him. It wasn't uncommon for me to be producing his reports until all hours of the morning while he watched TV. I had given up on my life ever being enjoyable again. My whole sense of individual identity was gone and I felt as though I barely existed.

Awareness and Seeking Help

A lesbian friend from the previous city I lived in sent me a book about SM [sado-masochistic] sub-cultures (one of her favourite things) that contained a chapter on the difference between an SM relationship and domestic violence. There was a checklist of questions to ask yourself to determine whether you were in an abusive relationship and when I found I was answering yes to almost everything, a crack appeared in the brainwashing and manipulation that had filled my head. I suddenly realised that I had to accept that I was in a domestic violence relationship.

I took the grand leap of confiding in someone I worked with about my situation and one afternoon, after Anthony threatened to "break both my legs" when I got home that night, this colleague generously lent me his spare room for a week while I "disappeared" from my home. During that week

I found a new place to live and, with a Gay and Lesbian Police Liaison Officer, I went to pick up my belongings and left.

A new phase of harassment and stalking that included a wide range of manipulations and threats (ranging from "Come back—I've changed!" to "If you have sex with another man I'll kill you and him") followed.

I decided to move to another city again and start a new life. It's taken a long time to feel confident about having sex again and the idea of getting emotionally close to someone is still shaky. I still feel wounded. But I've learnt some really important lessons about violence and the difference between control and love and I'm slowly working off the debt I left the relationship with. Day by day, I am rediscovering who I am. The most important thing for me now is that I am safe, I control my own life and I don't live each day terrified of going home.

Can My Abusive Wife Really Change?

Kevin

In the following selection, a man known only as Kevin admits to an online psychotherapist that his wife has verbally abused him for several years. As Kevin relates, her abuse became controlling as she demanded to know his whereabouts and sought to limit his interactions with family and friends. After compiling a mental list of numerous incidents, Kevin told his wife he no longer loved her, and the couple started marriage counseling. While his wife owned up to her behavior and stopped the abuse, the author asks the psychotherapist whether she believes an abuser can really change.

I married my wife 4 years ago and lived with her for a year before that. While we were dating she confided in me that her stepfather had sexually molested her for several years. I also learned that her biological father had not spoken to her in ten years and her mother verbally and emotionally abused her (and still does). I was young, self-assured and felt I had the strength to handle anything, so I married her.

After we were married, I noticed that she began to speak to me a little more harshly than before. She would order me to do chores or demand I be home at a certain time and if I was slightly late I got a verbal lashing to beat the band. As our marriage continued, she became much more demeaning in her comments. She would constantly tell me that I couldn't survive without her, she didn't know how I made it this far, my mother obviously didn't do a good job raising me since I didn't know how to do anything.

I remember one time I was listening to one of my favorite bands downstairs and she charged downstairs and started yell-

Kevin, "Husband Abuse Is No Different than Wife Abuse," Dr. Irene's Verbal Abuse Web site, www.drirene.com, September 26, 1999. Reproduced by permission.

ing at me. She said, "I can't believe you are listening to this s**t you go****n redneck. I'm so embarrassed of you. I hope none of the neighbors heard this s**t. I don't ever want to hear this s**t again. You're such an embarrassment to me." This was one of many incidents that took me aback.

Limiting Contact with Family and Friends

She also began controlling where and whom I saw. Whenever I wanted to go see my parents she would make it very clear that she did not want to go. She would pout, yell, scream and threaten not to go to my parent's house. I would finally convince her to make the trip and while we were there she made everyone miserable. She would disappear upstairs, not participate in with my family. My family would try to get her involved with events playing games, taking her (and me) out to eat and embracing her as my wife and a family member. She would have no part of it. In fact, if I wanted to play a card game while we were at my parent's house, she would do something that would force me to stop playing and attend to her. If I continued to play, she would let me know how horrible a person I am. She would tell me how much she hated my parents and tell me that I obviously loved them more than her. She just hoped that the umbilical cord would be cut soon, so I would learn to stand on my own.

When my son was born this year, she told me to call my parents and tell them not to come and see their grandson. This outraged me. I told her that she would have to do it, because I would not deprive my parents of meeting their grandson and that family would be an important part of his life. She fortunately did not make the phone call, but she was clearly agitated that they came up.

She also keeps me from doing things with my friends. If I want to go play golf, go out to a ball game or participate in any event with my friends, she tells me that I obviously like my friends better than her and sends me on a guilt trip. I once took a half-day off work to play golf with my co-workers. I had told her that I was going to do this and that I would be home as soon as I was done. I returned home at 5:30 that evening, which is about an hour before I normally get home. She started yelling at me, telling me how inconsiderate I was for not getting home sooner. She figured I wasn't coming home at all and wished I hadn't. She's not sure our marriage is going to work and we should get a divorce. After taking this for awhile, I stopped doing things with my friends. It seemed better to avoid the yelling than to take it.

Can She Change?

These are only isolated incidents of my life with my wife. Over the last four years I have compiled quite a mental list of incidents. I don't think my life is as bad as many of your other respondents. She has only struck me once out of anger and did stop giving me "love pats" after I repeatedly asked her to stop hitting me, but I feel like I have taken a lot of abuse throughout the years.

Here is the crux of my e-mail. About six months ago I told my wife I no longer love her and we began marriage counseling. Through it all she has stated that she now realizes what she has done is wrong, and will never do it again. In fact, for the most part she has been nice to me. Is it possible that she is truly changing?

CHAPTER 2

Family Violence
Affects Others Outside
of the Family

A Doctor Confronts Spousal Abuse in an Elderly Couple

Clif Cleaveland

In the following article, physician Clif Cleaveland recounts his experience in dealing with a domestic violence situation involving an elderly couple. As Cleaveland states, he slowly came to recognize that one of his older patients was beating his wife when the pair showed up for regular doctor visits. His attempt to intervene was rebuffed by both the wife and her family, who made it clear that this was a family affair. Cleaveland is an internal medicine physician in Chattanooga, Tennessee. He is past president of the American College of Physicians and author of Healers & Heroes: Ordinary People in Extraordinary Times.

She accompanied her husband on each visit to the office. He leaned heavily upon his cane while she supported him from his other side. Once in the examining room, she guided him carefully to his seat and stood behind his chair.

He was 75. A big-boned man with silver hair, his joints were no longer able to cope with his considerable weight. He required a few moments after he sat down before he could respond to my greeting and inquiry of how he felt. I never witnessed a smile. His voice, like his mood, was deep with dark undertones. Time and smoking had weakened his heart, and he struggled for breath between sentences. His hands rested atop the straight, heavy, gnarled cane held between his legs.

His replies were gruff and spoken loudly, perhaps because of impaired hearings, perhaps to assert a certain dominance in our exchanges.

I was far too young to serve as his physician. He tolerated me because his own physician of many years had died and I, being relatively new to the community, was available. His wife had insisted that he come to me.

When I asked a question concerning his health, he would say, "Tell him," nodding to his wife, who would then answer my question in some detail. So the interview would proceed. Only with great difficulty and much lifting could my nurse and I assist him to an examination table. He resented our effort; consequently, most of his examinations occurred while he sat. His manner ranged from grumpy to foul. The few words he spoke were spewed in burst, while he kept his eyes fixed upon me the entire visit. He predicted, in advance, that my prescriptions would not work. He reported side effects with the medications that he agreed to take.

The challenge with such a patient is, of course, to win him over, to establish some basis for at least neutral, if not cordial exchange. I never achieved even neutrality. Typical, a visit began with the recitation of recent symptoms and observations by his wife, a thin, reserved lady, with graying hair and fair skin. Her quiet nature contrasted sharply with that of her husband. Inquiries to the patient brought little additional information. After checking his blood pressure, heart, and lungs, I reviewed his medications. He complained if expected to return in less than three or four months. His wife and I helped him to his feet. Disdaining the offer of a wheelchair, he slowly and painfully made his way along the hallway to the exit.

Bruises and Excuses

One visit was different. The old man asked if I would "check [his] old lady." His wife hesitated, stating that nothing was wrong and, besides, she had no time for a check-up. Nevertheless, we scheduled time for her visit. On the appointed day her husband waited outside. She provided little information. Her answers were quietly delivered; she avoided my eyes and looked at the floor. She had osteoarthritis, and her blood pressure was mildly elevated. After listening to my recommendations, she thanked me and departed.

Some months later, when the old man came for his examination, his wife seemed even more reticent than usual. She held her head turned slightly away from me. As I stood at the end of the examination, I could see bruises over her cheek and forehead, which facial powder could not conceal.

"What happened to your face?" I asked.

"I ran into a door when I got up to go to the bathroom," she replied.

I asked, "Would you like for me to check you?"

"That won't be necessary," she said.

Another visit ended.

A few weeks later, when she came to the office for her appointment, I noted old and new bruises on her left arm and neck. I asked her to slip into an examination gown. She declined. She blamed the bruises on a fall down back porch steps. The footing had been slippery.

I asked if she had experienced dizziness or vertigo. She had not. She declined further examination.

I called the couple's son, a physician in a nearby community, to ask if he had noted any problems with his mother's equilibrium when he had last visited. He reported that, from his vantage point, his mother's health had shown no recent changes.

A visit or two later, the old man seemed in a mood far blacker than before. His wife wore a long-sleeved blouse. Her muted voice seemed somewhat tremulous. There was puffiness about her eyes, and one cheek was swollen.

She denied that anything was wrong and recited, as always, her husband's complaints.

At the end of the meeting I asked my nurse to assist the old man to the waiting room.

"Excuse us for a moment, I need to talk to your wife," I explained.

An Anxious Admission

Reluctantly, she agreed to remain behind. I invited her to sit. She looked impassively at the floor. I asked to examine her face, where once again powder incompletely camouflaged bruises.

"Let me see your arms," I said.

She did not resist as I unbuttoned the cuffs and rolled her sleeves upward. Multiple bruises, both old and new, were apparent on both arms. A large hematoma swelled her left upper arm. She declined further examination.

I looked at her. "Something is going on here. Is someone beating you?"

She shook her head but began to weep quietly, her head bowed, hands and knees tightly clamped together.

"Is it your husband?"

Again, she shook her head, "No."

Stymied, I urged that she let me call her son or involve a social worker from Family and Children's Service to help us.

"You mustn't tell anyone," she said.

"It is your husband then," I said.

This time she nodded affirmatively.

"With his cane?" I asked.

She nodded affirmatively once again and rose to leave.

I tried again. "You must let me help you."

She declined any assistance. She begged me to remain silent. Her husband was old and sick, and she had to care for him. Illness made him do cruel things. She could not be deterred from leaving, after seeing to her face, re-applying facial powder, and gathering her composure.

Mind Your Own Business

I left word at her son's office for him to telephone me upon his return from hospital duties. When he called at midday I indicated that we needed to meet to discuss a confidential and urgent matter. He was terribly busy. Could we not discuss the matter now?

I reviewed my observations for the previous two years and the denouement of that morning.

"This is a family matter. You mind your own damned business." He hung up.

I phoned the battered wife the next day. She stated that she was fine, and that she neither wanted nor needed any help. The family would take care of its own problems. She reminded me that her husband was quite ill and in need of her care. I listed ways in which she could obtain help, but she seemed little interested. She must hang up because her husband became upset if she spoke over the phone too long.

I never saw either of the physician's parents again as patients.

After a long interval I read the brief obituary of the old man. I wondered what had happened to his wife. I never saw her son or any family member from whom I could learn of her fate.

A Recent Encounter

Years later, during the national debate on health care reform, I addressed a group of senior citizens on the issue. After my remarks, while cookies and coffee were passed around the room, several members of the audience pressed their questions informally. The final person to greet me was the old man's widow.

She had aged surprisingly little. Her hair had whitened. Eyes that once had reflected the fear of a deer caught in headlights now seemed calm and alert. Her speech was crisp. She remained slender and moved easily.

She thanked me for my remarks. We engaged in safe chitchat about children and grandchildren. She visited regularly among her circle of friends and was active in her church and in Senior Neighbors.

When I asked her how she had been she said, "Just fine." But as she turned to leave, she paused for a moment and asked, "You never told anyone, did you?"

I smiled, and deferred an answer. She turned away to re-join the larger group in the social wind-down after a doctor's talk.

I know now of the pernicious extent of domestic violence. I have seen it many times and in unexpected settings. Were I to encounter the old man with a cane and his wife today, I would suspect his beatings much earlier. If the son declined intervention, I would call without hesitation the domestic violence hotline sponsored by my community's Family and Children's Service.

I wonder what became of the cane? Was it buried with the old man? Is it in the closet or garage? Was it simply thrown out?

A Victim of Domestic Violence Faces Workplace Discrimination

Shonnetta Collins

In 1995 Shonnetta Collins and her son were taken hostage by her abusive ex-husband. In the selection that follows, Collins relates how seven years later she felt concern about her husband's upcoming release from jail. She sought help and followed the given advice to obtain legal help, seek a restraining order, and to inform her workplace. The bank where she worked called a meeting, in which Collins believed more concern was expressed for the workplace than for her situation. After her husband was released from jail, someone—perhaps Collins's ex-husband— made a disturbing phone call to the bank manager. Collins was notified and, soon after, was fired. Shonnetta Collins now works as an advocate with Faith House in Louisiana, an organization providing outreach and shelters for women and children victims of domestic violence.

In November 2002 I started on a journey to protect myself and my son from further abuse at the hands of my ex-husband. I wanted to make sure that when he got out of jail he would have strict visitation with our son. He was in jail for an incident in August 1995 where he held my son and me hostage for 9 1/2 hours. He would be getting out on good behavior in January or February 2003, and I wanted to be prepared.

I attended a parole board meeting late in 2002 where a board member warned me that if my ex-husband did not change and if she was me, the day he got out she would move

Shonnetta Collins, "Discrimination Against Battered Women in the Workplace," *The Voice: The Journal of the Domestic Violence Movement*, Fall 2004, pp. 9–10. Reproduced by permission.

away as far as she could. At this same meeting, the police officer who was shot during the hostage situation stated that a condition of his parole should be to keep him out of the town where I was living. I had been through enough already so I shouldn't be the one to have to move.

Roadblocks in Seeking Help

Later in the hearing, I asked about his rights to see his son. A parole board member said that I would have to get a lawyer to get custody. After the hearing I contacted legal aid to ask for some advice. Legal aid told me that I could also go to Faith House, a domestic violence program, and also try to get a restraining order.

I called Faith House and met with the advocate, but she did not understand why legal aid sent me there since I did not need to go into hiding. She stated that I needed to tell my employer what was going on. I did, and my journey started to turn into a nightmare.

In early December 2002 I met with the judge in my parish to try to get a restraining order, which was denied because my ex-husband was not a threat to me. Coincidentally, this was the same judge who sentenced my ex-husband for the hostage incident. I felt like doors were being continuously shut in my face. I was running out of options so I thought back to the parole board meeting. I wanted to make sure that a condition of his parole was that he could not live in the same town where I was living. I called the parole board office and spoke with a victim advocate who said she would check on his parole conditions and get back to me.

When she called me back she read the conditions over the phone to me, which stated that he could not live in the town where I was living; he had to go through counseling, and had to stay away from my son and me. I was relieved, but my nightmare was far from over.

Work Calls a Meeting

At a bank branch where I worked, my manager wanted to set up a meeting to discuss my situation. I was questioned several times by my manager and remember feeling that it seemed like I would have to start looking for another job. My manager appeared to be more concerned about this situation than I was. Finally, a meeting was scheduled for January 10th, 2003 with the Attorney General's Office (who was supposed to be providing domestic violence training to my workplace), my bank's security department, human resources, a district manager, an operations manager, a Faith House advocate, the chief of police, and a bank lawyer.

Thirty minutes into the meeting a manager came out and asked me for my ex-husband's probation officer's phone number. I told her that I did not feel comfortable that they were having a meeting about me and that I was not invited. Then, she invited me to the meeting where the lawyer stated that they were all there to help me. The police chief told me that even though all these people were there to help me, I would have to take some action on my own. The first phone call I got, he instructed me, I would have to report it to the authorities.

Later that day my manager asked my co-workers how they felt about the situation with me. Everyone was OK with it, and all they wanted was a picture of my ex-husband so they could recognize him if he came to the bank. Before the day was over, everyone had a picture of my ex-husband. One of my co-workers told me that she was not as concerned about herself as she was for me.

I thought everything was going to be fine with this situation and continued doing my job as I always had. I was always on time for work and had an excellent work performance. What happened next turned out to be a big surprise.

My Ex-Husband Gets Released

My ex-husband was released on February 4th, 2003 and I received a phone call from his mother saying that my ex-husband was home and he wanted to know if he could speak to his son. A million thoughts started running through my head—the system had failed again—why was he in the town where I lived? I later learned that the parole board didn't get the conditions of his release to him in time. I allowed him to speak to his son and picked up another phone to listen to their conversation. He didn't say anything out of the way on the call, and I hesitated on calling the police. Finally, late that night I reported the call to the police in the town where I lived and the town where I worked.

The next day I reported to work, and the minute I clocked in my manager told me that they received a strange call. A man called and asked if I worked there and then wished me a blessed day. I figured, as did the manager, that it might have been my ex-husband, but there was no way to know for sure. The bank never bothered to trace the call. My manager called in a district manager to discuss the situation and they called me into the office a number of times that day. They also called in all the co-workers one at a time. They didn't make a decision about what to do with me and they told me that they might ask me to take a leave of absence for a while.

I was not happy about having to take a leave of absence, but it was better than having to quit or be fired. I had worked there for [more than one year] and [had] busted my butt to get where I was today. I wondered why they couldn't transfer me to one of the other bank branches.

Finally, they decided to suspend me with pay for the next two days until they figured out what they were going to do with me. By the end of the second day, they called me and asked if I could meet with them on Monday. On Monday they informed me that they decided to terminate me from my job, due to the best interests of the company.

A Classmate Fights
to Free a Friend Imprisoned
for Domestic Murder

Jennifer Gonnerman

In the selection that follows, reporter Jennifer Gonnerman tells of Joe Church, a man who attended his twentieth high school reunion only to find a popular classmate named Shelley has been sentenced to 15 years in prison for killing her violent husband. After hearing the story of Shelley's violent marriage, Church starts a clemency campaign to free her and other battered women inmates who face long sentences. Jennifer Gonnerman is a staff writer for the Village Voice *where she reports on the criminal justice system. She is the author of* Life on the Outside: The Prison Odyssey of Elaine Bartlett.

Joe Church had not even planned to go to his 20th high school reunion. At the last minute, he changed his mind and dropped by the Irish bar in downtown St. Louis, where 70 or 80 classmates from Mercy High School had gathered. Back in the mid-1970s, Joe had been the sort of student who showed up for school late and left early, a regular visitor to the discipline office. By the time of the reunion in the summer of 1997, he had a wife, four children, and a job as a stockbroker at Morgan Stanley.

After half an hour of drinking and mingling, Joe spotted Shelley Povis' cousin. In high school, Shelley had been pretty and popular; she had a spot on the football cheerleading squad and friends in every clique. She and Joe had never been close, but he remembered her as always smiling, always fun to be around.

"Where's Shelley?" he asked.

Jennifer Gonnerman, "The Unforgiven," *Mother Jones*, vol. 30, July–August 2005, pp. 38–43. Copyright 2005 Foundation for National Progress. Reproduced by permission.

"She's in prison," her cousin said.

Joe hadn't seen Shelley since graduation; the news stunned him. What sort of crime could she possibly have committed? Drugs? Bad checks? Shoplifting?

"She killed her husband," her cousin said.

Joe stayed at the reunion for a couple hours, then drove back to his house in the suburbs. Alone in his car, he tried to make sense of the news. A few days later, he sent Shelley a note and shortly after spoke with her on the phone. Shelley told him that she'd married an alcoholic who had abused her throughout their 14-year marriage. Three years ago, she'd confessed to killing him; a judge had sentenced her to 15 years in prison. "I was really taken aback with the whole thing," Joe says. "It was just hard to believe that, one, she could kill somebody, and two, under those circumstances she could've ended up in prison."

Eventually, one Saturday, Joe drove two and a half hours across the state to visit Shelley in prison; the next week, back in his office, he started making calls. He spoke with Shelley's mother, her former boss, the police. There was no doubt that Shelley had endured many years of beatings. The photos taken by the police after her arrest showed a woman he barely recognized, her face purple and black. "You don't have to look at those pictures very long to realize that something terrible was happening," he says. "How does a guy look at her and say, 'You're a murderer.' I just didn't understand."

Launching a Clemency Campaign

One of the first people Joe called was Colleen Coble, head of the Missouri Coalition Against Domestic Violence. He had dated her one summer when they were teenagers, but they hadn't spoken in 10 or 15 years. On the phone, he was full of questions about how to launch a clemency campaign: "What are we going to do? How much money do I need to raise? Who do we need to contact?" His zeal did not surprise her.

"He has a finely honed sense of right and wrong," she says, "and in that sense is the good Catholic boy his parents raised."

Joe moved quickly. He expanded his mission, compiling a list of women who might be good candidates for clemency. Then Colleen got a meeting for them with Governor Mel Carnahan's legal counsel. They were told that if they could gather more information about these women's cases, the governor would take a look at them. She contacted local law schools, and the Missouri Battered Women's Clemency Coalition was created. Soon every law school in the state had joined. Professors took up the cause in legal clinics, assigning students to reinvestigate cases of women who were in prison for killing their abusers.

One of the successes of the domestic violence movement has been its ability to publicize the plight of battered women serving prison time for crimes related to their abuse. Since 1978, the nation's governors have granted clemency to more than 125 women convicted of killing (or ordering the killing of) their abusers. . . .

Shelley's Story

While Joe Church was the catalyst for Missouri's latest clemency movement, his own priority was always the same: to get clemency for Shelley. Neither he nor the lawyers he had enlisted had any idea how long their fight would go on. All they really had was an unshakable belief that Shelley and many other women who had killed their abusers never deserved the harsh punishments they'd received.

Shelley Povis grew up in St. Ann, a blue-collar suburb west of St. Louis. When she was 17 and a senior at Mercy High, she began dating Rodney Hendrickson. She liked the fact that he was almost four years older. He hung out with her uncle and cultivated a bad-boy persona, growing his hair long and zooming around town on a motorcycle. According to the neighborhood grapevine, he had smacked around his last girlfriend.

Shelley's mother, Mickie, tried to dissuade her from dating him, but Shelley wouldn't listen. "He's really not a bad guy," she said.

Shelley and Rodney got married in 1980, when she was 21. She worked as a waitress; he got a job with the gas company. From the beginning, he kept her under surveillance. He would check on her all the time, calling or stopping by her job to make sure she was there. He also paid close attention to her appearance. If he thought another guy was checking her out, he'd get angry. Soon he was picking out her clothes for her— always modest items that would discourage other men. "I thought it was kind of neat," Shelley recalls. "I thought, wow, this guy wants to pick out my clothes. He really loves me."

Rodney was a heavy drinker, and when he got drunk he could become aggressive. Occasionally he would smack Shelley, or grab her and shake her. "A lot of it I thought was my fault," she says. It was impossible to predict when he'd lose his temper. She could be sitting next to Rodney watching television, and the next thing she knew he would be hitting her. After each fight, he apologized and tried to win her back. "He'd buy me gifts and flowers," she says. "There would be periods when he would treat me like a queen."

Moving Out

Eight years into the marriage, Shelley decided she'd had enough of Rodney's drunken rages. By now they had three children. She moved out, taking the children with her.

At first Rodney didn't know where she'd gone, but after four weeks he tracked her down at a shelter for battered women. She walked out the back of the shelter one day, and there he was, sitting in his truck. "You need to come home now," he told her. "If you don't go in there and get your stuff, I'm going to go in and get it." As usual, he made promises about how he had changed, how he was drinking less, how he wouldn't hit her anymore. Shelley and the children moved back into their house.

In the years that followed, Rodney warned Shelley never to run away from him again. "He told me if I ever left again, he would hunt me down," she says. She knew him well enough not to take this threat lightly. When she'd been at the shelter, he'd called her mother all the time, begging for information about where she was. Shelley worried that if she ever left Rodney again, she'd put not only herself and the children at risk, but her mother, too.

She hid these fears from her family, just as she had hidden the evidence of Rodney's abuse. She tried hard to project the image of a happy marriage, avoiding her relatives whenever she had a black eye or a bruise. "When we had a barbecue planned and I talked to her the day before, she'd say, 'Yeah, I'm going to bring the potato salad.' And everything was fine," her mother recalls. "That would be Saturday. And Sunday morning she'd call and say one of the kids was sick, or she was sick, or she just didn't show up."

The Stresses Mount

During the summer of 1993, the Missouri and Mississippi rivers overflowed. It was the most devastating flood in recent history, and damaged more than 55,000 homes, including Rodney and Shelley's. The entire interior of their house was destroyed, filled with slime and river water. Now they had four children and nowhere to live. They moved into Shelley's mother's basement for a few months, then into a tiny apartment, which was all they could afford. The stress mounted. Shelley and the children spent hours in emergency relief lines, trying to get free clothes or building materials. Rodney worked days driving a delivery truck, then at night rebuilding the house.

In November 1993, Shelley got a job as a weight-loss consultant. One day she showed up with a bruise stretching from one ear, across her throat, and all the way to her other ear. Another time her boss saw a dark spot the size of a dinner plate on Shelley's thigh. At first Shelley blamed her own clum-siness, but eventually she told the truth. When her boss urged her to leave Rodney, Shelley said she was afraid that if she did, he would hunt her down and kill her.

Shelley and Rodney moved back into their house in the summer of 1994, after living elsewhere for nearly a year. By now, they never seemed to have any good days anymore. Rod-ney had stopped trying to woo her back with gifts every time he hit her. "I wouldn't even get an 'I'm sorry,'" she says.

"None of You Are Leaving"

One day in the fall of 1994, he threatened her with a hunting knife. Afterward she hid the knife; Rodney became furious. "He had me up against the wall, choking me, telling me that I better have his knife when he got home from work or he was going to kill me." she says. Shelley pleaded with him to let her leave with the kids, but her words only made him more angry. "None of you are leaving," he said. "I'd rather see you all dead than leave."

Then 11-year-old daughter, Ashley, overheard this argu-ment. After Rodney left the house to go to work, Ashley said something Shelley found very disturbing. "She told me that he would come in and go to the bathroom when she was in the bathtub and watch her," Shelley says.

The following week, on October 29, Shelley drove to Kmart and bought a 12-gauge shotgun.

Rape, Murder and Lies

When police officers walked into the Hendrickson home at 2:45 a.m. on October 31, 1994, they found Shelley in her nightgown, curled up in the fetal position on the floor. She had a swollen eye, a bruise on her forehead, and tears running down her cheeks. Tied to one of her wrists was a piece of rope. Ashley was on the couch next to her; the three other children were in their rooms. In the master bedroom, the officers found Rodney facedown on the bed. Blood spattered the wall next to him. One of his eyeballs was on the floor. There was a gunshot wound in the back of his head.

At first Shelley insisted a pair of masked men had broken in, tied her to the bed, and shot Rodney. Three hours later, hunched over a table in an interrogation room at the police station, she confessed to the murder. Earlier that night, she explained, after the children had gone to sleep, Rodney had grabbed her by the hair, smashed her head against the headboard, and tied her wrists to the bed. Then he raped her. After he fell asleep, she'd freed herself and reached under the bed to get the shotgun.

An autopsy later revealed that at the time of his death Rodney had a large amount of cocaine in his system. The police found the shotgun in the basement, in a portion still filled with water from the flood 16 months earlier. They found the rest of the ammunition in another part of the basement, hidden in a box with Christmas lights.

Too Many False Stories

During the police interrogation. Shelley admitted lying about more than just the masked men. Two days earlier she'd called 911 and made a false report, claiming that someone had stolen her new shotgun. She had fabricated this story, she insisted, to steer Rodney off course if he found out she'd purchased a weapon. Why had she decided to buy a gun in the first place? "To protect myself," she said.

The masked men, the stolen gun, the false report she filed with the police—all of the made-up stories undermined Shelley's credibility in the minds of the officers. "Based on these circumstances, I told Michelle that I was having a hard time believing anything she told me," one sergeant wrote in his report. To someone who knew her history of abuse, Shelley's fabrications might have looked very different—evidence of her desperation as she increasingly felt her life was in danger.

Shelley was taken to the county jail and charged with first-degree murder. Her bail was set at $1 million. Six weeks later, during a preliminary hearing, an expert on battered women testified that Shelley had endured nearly 20 years of abuse and that she was not a threat to society. In another county, a better understanding of the psychology of domestic violence victims (combined with the way Shelley's face looked when she was arrested) might have convinced the prosecuting attorney to charge her with a less serious crime—manslaughter, say, instead of murder. But the prosecutors in St. Charles County, a conservative area outside St. Louis, did not budge.

Shelley's children—ages 11, 8, 7 and 5—moved in with one of Rodney's sisters. Shelley's first choice, her own sister, had no room in her house since she already had five children of her own. Shelley spent the next two years in the county jail, trying to figure out what to do. If she went to trial and lost, she'd likely spend the rest of her life in prison. In the end, she decided to plead guilty to second-degree murder in exchange for a 15-year prison sentence. She would be eligible for parole in about 13 years. By then all four of her children would have grown up without her.

Eleven Good Candidates

Professsors and students at four law schools across Missouri worked throughout most of 1999 and 2000 preparing clemency applications. They sorted through dozens of cases and came up with 11 women they thought were good candidates. All met the same criteria: They had a history of domestic violence; they had been convicted of killing (or ordering the killing of) their batterers; they had received lengthy prison sentences; and they had exhausted all their legal appeals.

Of the 11 women, 5 had life sentences, 3 had to serve 50 years before they were eligible for parole, I had a 20-year sentence, and 2 (including Shelley) had received 15 years. The clemency petitions contended that the "presence of prolonged and sustained abuse" should have reduced the women's culpability in the eyes of prosecutors and resulted in less severe punishments.

"These women are not what have been described as your 'typical murderers,'" wrote Jane Aiken, a professor at Washington University School of Law, in a legal brief filed with the petitions. "They did not act with 'cold hearts': their acts are better characterized as final acts of desperation in the context of severe physical and sexual violence inflicted upon them."

In this clemency campaign, Shelley played a crucial role. She recruited many of the women, including her friend Carlene Borden, who'd been locked up since 1978 in connection with her boyfriend's murder of her abusive husband. Of the 11 women represented by the team of law professors, Carlene had been imprisoned the longest. Another candidate was Ruby Jamerson, who had been sent to prison in 1989 for asking her son and his friend to kill her abusive husband.

Twenty-one Letters of Support

Much has changed since the 1970s and 1980s, when Carlene and Ruby were convicted. Now police officers are more likely to arrest an abusive husband when his wife calls the police. When a woman is charged with killing her batterer, the defense team often includes an expert on domestic violence. And judges are much more likely to allow testimony about past abuse. Indeed, as the clemency petitions pointed out, women accused of killing their abusers in the 1970s and 1980s would likely receive less prison time today for the same crime.

To bolster Shelley's clemency application, her legal team collected 21 letters of support from members of her family and 36 from friends and former classmates at Mercy High. Nobody from Rodney's family wrote on her behalf, but Rodney's sister-in-law Melissa did write to Shelley's lawyers, trying to dissuade them. "The fact of the matter is that Michelle Hendrickson is a murderer," she wrote. "I don't feel that after planning and premeditating a murder and shooting her husband in the head with a deer slug that she should be released after just 6 years."

In the summer of 2000, Governor Carnahan was running for a seat in the U.S. Senate. Hopes were high that he might grant clemency to a group of women right before he left office, when elected officials are more likely to make this sort of politically risky decision. Then, on October 17, 2000, Carnahan died in a plane crash. The possibility that Shelley and the rest of the women would be let out of prison early suddenly seemed much less likely. . . .

Clemency Denied

At the end of 2004, Shelley received a letter stating that her request for clemency had been denied. There was no explanation. Now she must wait three years before she can reapply. "That's one of the ridiculous things about this case," says Marie. "It literally sat on the governor's desk for almost five years, so that was five years of wasted time."

One morning this spring, Shelley, who is now 45, told her story to a reporter while seated in the parole room at a prison in Vandalia, Missouri. She wore a gray inmate uniform and two crosses, one on a chain around her neck and another pinned to her collar. She still has curly blond hair, but now it's thinner on top. Both her mother and grandmother had breast cancer, and two years ago Shelley discovered a lump in one of her breasts. She recalls that it took her five or six months to get treatment. Joe and her mother called the prison regularly, trying to speed up the process. "You could be jeopardizing her life," Joe would say. Eventually Shelley had a lumpectomy, then chemotherapy and radiation.

These days, Shelley no longer sees bruises or black eyes when she looks in the mirror, but she can still see faint scars on her wrists, reminders of the rope burns she got when Rodney tied her to the bed. Though 11 years have passed since that last night with him, the memories are fresh in her mind. "I can still smell the smells," she says—sweat, gunpowder, blood. "And I can still hear the sounds. I can still feel the hits. I can still feel every time my head hit that headboard. I can still feel the burns on my wrists."

Her Children Struggle

From behind the walls of prison, she tries to be a mother to her children, who are now 22, 18, 17, and 15. She calls them every Sunday evening at Rodney's sister's house, and her mother brings the youngest one to see her every month. But more than a year has passed since Shelley last saw her oldest child, Ashley. A few years ago, Ashley got into an abusive relationship, started using drugs, and got arrested. "Nobody knew where she was for over a year," Shelley says. "She was living in a car." The hardest part of being locked up, says Shelley, has been watching her kids struggle without her.

To boost Shelley's spirits, Joe reminds her of what they've accomplished over the last eight years: Two women will soon be freed, including 74-year-old Shirley Lute. "This lady was destined to die there," Joe says. "As I keep telling Shelley, had she not gone to prison, there's a good chance Shirley Lute may never have gotten out." Joe is planning a barbecue this summer to celebrate Shirley's release.

Shelley is not eligible for parole until 2007, when she will have served 85 percent of her sentence. Most likely she will leave behind Carlene, Ruby, and the rest of the women who joined the clemency campaign. Unless a sympathetic governor intervenes, they are destined to grow old in prison.

CHAPTER 3

Ending the Violence

A Police Detective Seeks Answers to Why He Beat His Wife

Duane Minard, as told to Tara McKelvey

Duane Minard was a successful police detective and a loving dad. He was also a wife beater. In the following article, Minard tells his story to reporter Tara McKelvey. Married for the third time to a woman he called perfect, Minard never expected to become abusive as he had in his earlier marriages. One day he exploded, but this time his battered wife called the police. Suspended from his job, he attended an intensive intervention program and slowly began to understand how his violent childhood and his police job reinforced beliefs that he could control other people with force. Determined to break the destructive patterns, he and his wife founded an outreach organization that provides domestic abuse victims with financial assistance, counseling, and other services. Tara McKelvey is a columnist and assistant life editor at USA Today.

I never imagined I could hurt a woman—until I did. I then spent years telling myself she deserved it. The first time I was 20, and my 18-year-old bride, Cheryl, slept with my best friend. When I found out, I felt so betrayed that I called her every demeaning name I knew. For seven years, I berated her, slapped her, and pushed her around. By attacking Cheryl, I felt like I had control over her and myself. She'd had an affair, I'd tell myself, and now I had to keep her in line.

When Cheryl left me, I didn't feel guilty or responsible. Instead I thought, Next time, I'll marry a woman who is strong enough to take it.

I met my second wife, Pam, at work, where I was a police detective and she was a sheriff's aide. She had an appealing combination of toughness and compassion. "Watch your head getting in the car," she'd say to the perpetrators we arrested. And yet, whenever one of these guys talked back to her, she put him in his place.

Pam and I got married—and that's when we started arguing. Our fights became physical: I'd shove her, she'd shove me back. I'd pull her hair, she'd pull mine. Aggression was normal to us; we had both grown up with it. We continued to mistreat each other for 10 years, until we finally agreed to divorce.

When I met Cesaria in 1999, I thought, Now this is a woman I could love. Sure, I had a history of losing my temper, but that was over. After all, I told myself, I wasn't the problem—it was the women I'd married. My first wife had cheated; my second wife had provoked me. There would be no reason to hurt Cesaria. She was perfect. She was a single mother, a private-school teacher, and an actress in community theater. She had her life together, and I adored her.

Then It Was Her Turn

For the first few years, life with Cesaria was wonderful. After we got married we moved in with her mother while our new house was being built. But one night in December 2001, Cesaria's ex-boyfriend stopped by unexpectedly—and I nearly ruined everything.

I stood, glaring, in the livingroom doorway as Cesaria invited him in, hugging him and kissing him on the cheek. As they sat down on the couch together, I felt a surge of fear. This guy was young, blonde, and blue-eyed; I was a 40-year-old Native American with brown eyes and black hair. How could Cesaria love me, compared with him? I knew she was going to run off with him.

Watching them, my fear and self-doubt turned to rage. I could feel veins pulsing in my neck. My hands were sweaty. I got tunnel vision. I'd never felt this way with Cesaria before.

Her ex didn't stay long, and after he left, I started an argument about his visit. But it went nowhere, so we just went to bed in silence.

At first, I lay there staring at the shadows on the wall. Then, suddenly, I exploded. I jumped on my wife—grabbing her, choking her, slapping her, pulling her hair.

"Duane!" Cesaria cried out, shocked. It was as if she was calling for my help—except I was the one attacking her.

You brought this on yourself, Cesaria, I thought. Out loud I threatened, "You don't have a good reason to live. I'm going to kill you." I wanted her to believe me, to be more scared than she'd ever been. Her fear would erase mine.

By the time I finished beating my tiny, 4'11" wife, she was bloody and bruised, I'd ruptured her eardrum and fractured her jaw. One of her ribs was torn away from the muscle.

At last, my anger was spent. I picked up my loaded gun and handed it over to her. "Here. Now it's even," I said. "You've got the gun, so let's have a discussion."

When Cesaria's eyes met mine, I recoiled. She looked so afraid. My other wives had always stared at me like, "You're such a jerk." But Cesaria's wounded look was heartbreaking. For once, I was unable to justify what I'd done.

Owning Up to the Abuse

I avoided Cesaria the next morning by going to work early. At around noon, she called to tell me she'd filed a report against me. I hung up. As a detective, I knew I was going to be arrested. The evidence was all over her face and body. I was about to lose everything—my wife, my career, my friends—and I'd done it with my own hands. I thought about killing myself. Or running away. I felt so guilty. I just wanted to hold Cesaria—and I couldn't.

But I didn't run. Before the day's end, I was sitting in jail. I spent four days there, thinking about what I'd done. Maybe I was to blame for my failed marriages. Maybe it wasn't the fault of the women in my life. On the day I was released, I went for a drive. My wife and children were gone, and as I stared at the stuffed animal and baseball glove in the backseat of my car—reminders of my family—I felt hopeless.

I was put on paid administrative leave following Cesaria's report, but my lawyer warned me, "Your law-enforcement career is over." I resigned and began working for a private investigator. I went about my life in a daze for two weeks—and then Cesaria called.

We agreed to meet at a Denny's at midnight. I was so nervous—l wanted her to trust me again. As I slipped into the booth, I noticed she was wringing her hands. Her cell phone was on the table.

She stared at me, searching. I held her stare, silently trying to tell her I knew I was wrong.

"Why did you hit me?" she asked.

"You were being disrespectful," I said, fumbling. "I felt like you were going to leave me, and I didn't want you to go."

"Uh-uh," she said sternly. "Why did you hit me?"

"No more angry outbursts," I promised. "No more shouting. Everything will be OK."

"No," she said. "I want you to tell me why."

"I don't have the answers," I finally admitted. "I need to find them." We ended up talking for hours.

Breaking the Patterns

Cesaria didn't give up on me. I entered a 52-week batterers' intervention program, and we both read books on domestic violence. Reading about how violence is passed down from father to son made me rethink my childhood. Some days, my dad used to open the door of our trailer home and shout obscenities, angry at the way he was treated in the "white man's world." Then he'd break down in tears. Many nights, he'd come home drunk. He'd slap me, throw me across the room, and then go looking for my mom. Those nights, I was really scared. I'd get angry and think, Someday I'm going to be big, and I'll get back at you.

After I grew up and left home, I thought of myself as a survivor of my childhood. But once I started reading about domestic violence, I realized that it wasn't enough to have survived. And my job with the police had only reinforced the notion that it was OK to control other people with force. It was all wrong. I had to break out of the pattern.

Cesaria agreed to a reconciliation, but she set firm ground rules. She drew up a contract stating that if I ever got violent again, she would get the house, the car, everything. We signed it in front of a notary public. As we rebuilt our relationship, Cesaria began formulating an idea. She wanted to help other victims of domestic abuse so that they'd never feel as alone as she had. She explained that after I'd beaten her, her friends and family didn't support her at all. I was surprised and sad— and I agreed that no woman should be shunned just because she's a victim of abuse.

Reaching Out to Help Others

Recently, Cesaria and I founded an outreach organization called Victory Over Domestic Abuse (VODA; voda4u@aol. com). At first, I stayed in the background while Cesaria set the agenda. But slowly, I started talking to women about why men hit. It was difficult trying to explain what I'd done, and what I was doing to ensure I never abused again. But in the end, it made me feel good to say, "I'm on the right track."

To date, VODA has provided nearly 300 victims of domestic violence with financial assistance, counseling, and other services. In addition, I've spoken about domestic violence to hundreds of men at local businesses and church groups. I haven't been abusive since that December two years ago—though sometimes when I'm frustrated, I find myself clenching my fists, ready to hit. But I resist the urge. Cesaria's attitude helps: If you're in a place where even hollering seems wrong, it's easier not to use violence.

I still don't have all the answers, but I know the questions need to be looked at in a hard light—every day. I used to train dogs on the police force, and I think of curing yourself of violence in the same way as getting over a dog bite. First, you have to open the wound and clean out any poisons. Then, the wound has to heal from the inside out. And I will always need to keep opening the wound in order to remain violence-free.

Taking a Stand against Abuse with the Help of My Boss

Lorel Stevens

Lorel Stevens finally left her twelve-year abusive relationship in 1999. In the following article Stevens relates how she, her husband, and five-year-old son stopped into her work after hours on a Saturday. A violent altercation ensued inside the workplace, but Stevens expected that no one in the near-empty offices noticed. Later, Stevens learned that her boss had witnessed the abuse and offered to help. His strong stance against domestic violence was pivotal in encouraging Stevens to find support and make the decision to leave the relationship. Lorel Stevens now works to end domestic violence through education, awareness and prevention. She cochairs SHARE, the survivors' group and speakers' bureau of the Arizona Coalition Against Domestic Violence. In 2003 she was appointed to the Governor's Commission for Prevention of Violence Against Women.

I was seventeen, a junior in high school, when I met him. He seemed so confident, secure, almost had a knowing arrogance in his attitude. He was so unlike me—reserved, shy and naïve. I wish I could have seen a snapshot of the future that day. I would have surely run the other way.

His manipulation and control was so subtle at first. It wasn't long before I was sucked in to the trap. I figured if I just tried a little harder, did or said something differently or loved him a little more that I could make him happy. Within about six months I had become more isolated from friends and family. His behavior moved from verbal abuse to physical attacks followed by profuse apologies and promises during this time as well. In our almost twelve years together the first

Lorel Stevens, "Taking a Stand," *The Voice: The Journal of the Domestic Violence Movement*, Fall 2004, p. 33. Reproduced by permission.

five and a half he was physically abusive and during the six years of our marriage he was verbally and emotionally abusive. It was not until after the physical abuse time was crossed again in front of our young son, that I knew there was no reason for me to try to hold the family together anymore.

A Violent Incident

On Saturday October 15[0], 1999 just two days before our sixth wedding anniversary, our lives were forever marked. The three of us, my then husband, our five-year-old son and myself were home deciding what to do for the day. My husband had remembered that I had recently received a bonus from my work and wanted to see the pay stub. I had left the stub locked in my desk drawer at work. He was furious about my leaving sensitive items at the office and insistent about retrieving it and thoroughly inspecting my desk to make sure I was not hiding anything from him. I tried to control this by letting him know that the employees were not to be in the building on the weekends and that my using my card to gain access would be tracked. He would not listen. He packed my son and I in the car and drove to my office building. Most offices were closed but there were cars in the parking lot and some office windows lit up. While rifling through my desk he had worked himself up into a frenzy, and started attacking me. He continued attacking and yelling at me all the way through the building, in the parking lot and all the way home as I drove. When we were walking in the house my husband says to our son, "Sometimes Mommy needs a spanking too."

Her Boss's Help

Our phone message light was blinking when we got inside. To our dismay my boss had witnessed part of the attack that occurred in the parking lot and wanted to contact the police. My husband had me call him back and make excuses and lie about it not happening before, to protect myself I did. Although I was able to talk my boss out of filing a police report he still came by the house to check on us. My boss assured me privately that no matter what decision I made about this that he would back me up. When I returned to work on Monday there was a newsletter on my desk from the Family Advocacy Center with a help line phone number on it. I decided to call. With the information and assistance from the Center and my employer I was able to come up with a safety plan, file a police report, get an order of protection, file for divorce, get my son and our things and leave.

The support I received along the way made the decision to leave a bit easier, successful and permanent. The stand my employer took against domestic violence was a strong one. It sends a strong message to all of us about our moral responsibility to step in and take action. Whether its offering to listen, providing information, contacting the authorities or getting involved in the community this is an issue that demands our attention. It is my personal endeavor to increase the awareness of domestic violence by sharing my experience with others for education and the prevention of this tragedy.

Breaking Free from My Abusive Children

Ana Sandor

*In this selection, a therapist and facilitator known as Ana San-
dor (not her real name), tells the story of the abuse she suffered
from her adopted son and daughter, who were diagnosed with
bipolar disorder and depression, respectively. After she and her
husband divorced, Sandor's two teenaged children became physically and verbally violent with her, leading to numerous visits
from the police and a growing distance in their relationship.
Sandor discusses what she has learned about parent abuse and
how people in abusive situations can take steps to change. Sandor has worked as an adjunct psychology professor and therapist
and now attends a doctorate level program in psychology.*

Allen and Charity were two older children adopted into a
military family. The adoptive parents did not have a com-
plete medical history; yet, both parents wanted to provide a
loving home environment regardless of their eventual divorce.

Life after divorce can be an adjustment, yet, the family
struggled to cope and develop a new nuclear family of Mom
and two children with contact from their father. Children
learn early to manipulate situations. Children learn to exercise
choice early in life; choice becomes a tool in their tool chest of
experience.

Allen and Charity are my children. As a new parent, I
wanted to love them and nurture them. They became my
world. As parents, we went through class after class to meet
the requirements for adoption. Yet, sometimes life is not fair
and you are dealt a hand that can be difficult. This was Allen
and Charity.

Ana Sandor, "Allen and Charity . . . The Beginning." Reproduced by permission.

The Abuse Begins

Allen and Charity were very frustrated with the divorce. Allen was diagnosed with bipolar disorder and Charity was diagnosed with depression. Yet, ultimately, it was an issue of choice that Charity exercised the first time she pulled a knife on me because she could not get her way. She was around 14 or 15 years of age and wanted to go out. She was unwilling to follow the house rules; so the answer was no. Setting limits and boundaries are a huge part of the parenting equation. This was not the first time that I said no to her; yet, this was the first time that she became violent. This was the first time that the sheriff met my children. It would not be the last time.

During the course of the next five years, the sheriff's department became intimately familiar with my children. My daughter entered therapy and overall stopped being physically abusive; yet, she became verbally abusive. In the end, she moved out at 18. Ironically, even my daughter could not handle the abuse heaped upon us by her brother.

Allen used his bipolar disorder as an excuse to become abusive. Violence is sometimes a part of the bipolar cycle in some; yet, others learn to exercise choice. Our family was in turmoil. Allen refused to accept the word "no" ever. Terrorization and manipulation became a method of control to Allen. He began punching holes in the walls and doors along with damaging his bedroom furniture.

Allen learned to use psychological abuse as a method of control. The taller he grew the more abusive he got. These acts culminated in 2001 and turned physical the first time that he laid a hand on me. Both he and his sister physically attacked me for denying a request. They attacked me on the stairs. I fell down two or three stairs injuring myself. They attempted to restrain me. I got away while calling 911. The sheriff had to restrain my son for the first of many times. I was a trained professional, a therapist, yet I could not effectuate a change in his behavior. The violence continued.

After Charity moved out in 2001 Allen's behavior became more erratic and more violent. In June 2002, Allen became angry because he was not permitted to go out. He became enraged and kicked in my bedroom door after I locked it. I was on the phone with the sheriff as he threatened to kill me. He figured out how to disconnect the house phone as I spoke with the Sheriff. Allen kicked my bedroom door off of the hinges as the sheriff's deputy's arrived to restrain my son. Allen was 17 and was terrorizing me in my own home. I replaced the bedroom door with a steel door for protection. I was terrified to live in my own home.

Allen was arrested as a juvenile and put on probation. He was ordered to make restitution for the damages. Allen was warned that if he did not meet the 90-day probationary period he would be incarcerated. Allen played the game until the Fall 2002. In late September Allen again violated a house rule; he became violent. I called 911. Allen spent two and a half weeks in a psychiatric ward. He was released back into my care as he was not quite 18. After his release, we were making plans to transfer Allen to his father's home. Allen made the choice to become violent. He cornered me in my bedroom and kicked in the steel door as he brandished a knife, disconnected my house phone, and would not permit me to leave the house. I eventually escaped to the garage with my car keys where I was again cornered. He had the knife. I ended up telling him to back away or I will hit him with the car door; my life was precious to me. He came towards me as I started the car backing away screaming for help. My neighbors called 911. This was the last time that my son ever abused me. This was the beginning of a life based upon my choices; I choose to live a life that does not include abuse. The boundary has been set and I will hold both of my children accountable for their behaviors and choices.

Recognizing the Signs

I have since learned that within society there is a form of abuse that is hidden within the context of the family structure; the abuse of a parent by the child(ren). These are children who pull knives on their parents because they are not permitted to go to the movie or who threaten to harm themselves because they do not get their way. It is a form of abuse that is under reported because of the stigma associated with being a "bad parent" or "you should be able to control your children"; or the belief that your children are "a reflection of your parenting style." Family history plays a huge role in the skills adults bring into the parent-child relationship; yet, family history does not completely account for choices executed by an adolescent or child. I believe that to abuse someone is a choice, a life altering choice.

Statistics show me that I am not alone—one in ten parents is assaulted by their children annually. The majority of the abuse occurs in single family homes with the mother being the primary victim of abuse. Boys are more apt to commit physical violence toward parents while girls are more apt to commit psychological and financial abuse. Parent abuse generally begins between the ages of 12–14 and peaks between ages 15–17.

At the core of all violence are the issues of power and control. Teens use power as a method of controlling their parents. Sometimes the parents surrender their role as an adult to the teen as a method of self-preservation. This leads to feelings of powerlessness and rage in response to family problems. I've read where children who are exposed to violence are most likely to engage in violence. Exposure to violence includes violence found in school, television, computer games, community violence, or a wider societal structure that reinforces violent interpersonal actions as the "norm" in relationships.

Society teaches children, especially boys, to be "macho" and emotionally void. Instead of addressing the emotions, children are taught by society to stuff their feeling away. What would happen if the parent peeled away the layers of emotions? Most likely, as I have found in my clinical practice, the parent would find that behind the aggression and defensive behavior is someone who is emotionally frightened and not having their needs met. The child feels powerless and experiences rage.

Treatment

With a skilled professional begin to assess the family context. Is there intergenerational abuse? Did the parent suffer abuse in a relationship as a child or adult? Did the parent spank their child or continues to spank their child? Regain control of the family by putting a name to the problem and then access counseling. Examine the emotional distance from each other in the family. Are the family members isolated from other friends and family? Do the parents avoid conflict by closing communication channels? What is the parent's perception of their life situation? Develop a safety plan.

If you are abusing your parents just stop the abuse. Seek help by speaking to a school counselor or another trained professional. If you are being abused by your children—seek help. Speak to a friend, your religious leader, social services, or a trained professional. There are many programs available for adolescents to participate in while still learning to be a part of the family. Be willing to do the ultimate act of tough love— you may have to remove your child temporarily from your home in order to survive and thrive as a family. Yet, sometimes you must accept the fact that you will never be able to do enough. You may have to move on.

Develop a strong support network. Learn who your neighbors are—parents tend to look out for each other. Be willing to step outside of your comfort zone and seek help. If the interventions are not working; be willing to put your abuser out of your home. Your safety and life may depend upon it.

A Mother Renounces a Pattern of Violence

Meri Nana-ama-Danquah

In the following selection, Meri Nana-ama Danquah relates how violence was a part of her life as a daughter in Ghana where corporal punishment was part of traditional African culture. The physical discipline and verbal abuse continued after she emigrated with her family to the United States when she was six. Later, Danquah entered her own abusive relationship and became pregnant but vowed to never continue the pattern with her young infant. One day, in frustration, Danquah approached her infant daughter to hit her for destroying a $10 cassette tape. In that instant, she decided to break the cycle of violence. She began a personal journey to explore and renounce her abusive history. Meri Nana-ama Danquah is a poet, journalist and the author of Willow, Weep for Me: A Black Woman's Journey through Depression.

The entire first year of motherhood for me was tainted by violence: physical violence, emotional violence, social violence. Giving birth itself seemed to be an act of violence. The landscape of my body became a battlefield during labor. There was excruciating pain, screaming, blood from the tearing of flesh, and well-earned scars, which, like tattoos, will be forever etched on my thighs and abdomen. I was plagued by an undiagnosed depression that debilitated me throughout the greater parts of both the pregnancy and my daughter's infancy. By the time my daughter, Korama, was born, the partnership between her father and me was crumbling. We had drained the pleasure fron our romance and were left with only harsh words and hardened hostility. On top of everything else, in April of

Meri Nana-ama-Danquah, from *Child of Mine*. Hyperion, 1997. Reproduced by permission of the author.

1992, the month of Korama's first birthday, Los Angeles was brought to its knees by racial injustice and riots. Indeed, Korama and I took a journey that year that lead us through fury and fear, through alarming confrontations with my past and necessary negotiations for a peaceful future.

In hindsight, I see now that I have always had a proclivity for turmoil and individuals who created or sustained it, as well as a predisposition to depression. This is a toxic combination for a new mother, but it was brewing in me long before I discovered I was going to have a baby. My own childhood was full of emotional disorder. I grew up in a household that mistook control and intimidation for love, the rush and intensity of anger for passion. There were never broken bones, just broken spirits, but we danced dangerously close to the threshold of domestic violence. And in the wake of our emotional wreckage, we concealed our pain with silence, retreated, like phantoms, behind facades.

A native of Ghana, I have lived in the United States since I was six years old and alternately embraced three disparate cultures: Ghanaian, mainstream American (read: white), and black American. My family strongly believed in traditional African values and principles such as the prerequisite respect of elders, the unspoken second-class citizenship of children, and the collective endorsement of corporal punishment. To not physically discipline one's children is akin to not feeding them three square meals or not providing them with an education. It is virtually unheard of. As a result, I spent my youth in blood-curdling fear of my parents' power. Their words—whatever words—were law. There was no freedom in my childworld to challenge or reject, no license to question. I held no rights that could be exercised without the threat of violence.

As it turned out, all that fear only translated into politeness, not sincere respect. No child of mine, I promised myself, would grow up the way I did. I wanted to have a relationship with my children based on love and genuine respect, not fear or obligatory deference. At the same time, though, I wanted to pass on to them the honor of heritage. I wanted them to eat the food and speak the languages of my primary culture. It is a classic desire: wanting to mold a child into something other than a reflection of yourself, while refusing (or simply not knowing how) to abandon the tools and models your parents used to shape you. My better judgement told me that it would be a difficult, if not, altogether impossible task, so at a very young age, I vowed to never become a mother.

Ironically, I was the first among my peers to get pregnant. At sixteen I had an abortion. At nineteen I had another. At twenty, I had a miscarriage two weeks after I found out I was, for the third time, pregnant. Had I not miscarried, I would have most likely had another abortion. The fourth and last pregnancy I carried the term. Like all the others, it was un-planned and, initially, unwanted. I was twenty-two years old, a college dropout who feared that having a child would mean forgoing an artistic career. I ultimately decided to go forward with the pregnancy more because of cryptic dreams and vague longings than any strict logic or rational sense.

There may be such a thing as a "perfect" or "right" time to have a child, but by anyone's standards the timing of my preg-nancy seemed all wrong. My boyfriend and I were still living together but we had reached an undeniable impasse in our re-lationship, we fought constantly, throwing insults, objects, and punches to injure one another. This was not the spirit in which Korama was conceived but until we split up, when she was eight weeks old, it was the tepid climate of our home. Given my history of low self-esteem and harmful liaisons, it was a climate in which I existed rather comfortably. I had never learned to expect anything more substantive than sex in a relationship, not even civility or consideration. Having a baby expanded my focus; it made me want to work things out in my life, especially with my boyfriend. I naively imagined that somehow our baby could bring us closer, if not erase the tension which was thick between us. I was wrong. The feuding persisted and eventually he threw me and the baby out of his home.

Korama and I moved into an apartment in a rundown building that I agreed to manage in exchange for free rent. I taught creative writing part-time, and more nights than I care to remember were spent working a phone sex line out of my home. A dense cloud of melancholy hung over my head. On my own, with a newborn, I began to reevaluate my decision to become a parent. *Did I make a mistake?* I wondered each night as I stared at the ceiling, swallowing worries. There was never enough money, and the only child-care assistance I received was from a small, makeshift support network of young, childless friends. Life began to seem too large and laborious to deal with.

Most of my time was devoted to obsessing about how much of a failure I thought I was. I felt as if I hadn't succeeded at anything in life—not in my education, not in my relationships, not in my literary ambitions. It was hard for me to move past all the guilt and self loathing. Caring for an infant was burdensome. It required more energy than the depression allowed me to give. I became afraid of failing at motherhood as well, and that was a thought I couldn't bear to consider.

Luckily, Korama was a low-maintenance infant. She rarely cried except when she needed to be nursed or diapered, and she slept soundly for long stretches of time. Mostly, she would just lie there next to me in bed and stare. Her look haunted me. I felt as if she sensed my ineptitude, knew in her tiny heart that she had been shortchanged by the heavens and granted a mother who was no more capable of dealing with the world than she. The life I had planned for Korama and me was all too quickly moving out of my reach.

When I think back to those days, what I recall most vividly is the enormous amount of rage and frustration I fought to suppress. While trying to maneuver around the guilt and resentment to access the love I knew I had for my daughter, *my* own potential for abuse was exposed and, to my surprise, I had been engaging in a constant and precarious flirtation with it. In August of that year [1992], when Korama was four months old, I had to file a domestic violence restraining order against her father. He had come to my house for a visit with his daughter that ended with him beating me.

It has been said that parents often raise their children to be all that they themselves could not or would not be. That is not the kind of parent I wanted to be. I had always hoped my child would inherit a few traits that genes alone could not translate. Traits like integrity, pride, perseverance, the spirit of compassion, and a strong sense of self. I wanted her to be familiar with the sound of her own laughter, but one is not able to give what one does not possess.

My turning point came on a frigid evening in January of 1992. Korama was nine months old. The depression had lifted ever so slightly, but I was still riding a flimsy seesaw of self-deprecating emotions. We were in the living room. Korama in one corner with her Christmas toys. I in another listening to my favorite cassette. I was flipping the tape over in the recorder when I caught the scent of burning food. Apparently I had forgotten to turn off one of the burners on the stove. I rushed into the kitchen. When I returned minutes later, Korama was crouched where I had been sitting, encircled by a spool of loose tape, the empty cassette still in her hand.

I could feel all the stifled rage traveling through every vessel in my body. I marched blindly toward her, ready to unleash it. My footsteps were heavy, thundering. Even the flesh on my palms was quivering in anticipation. I was no less than two yards away when I stared into her pupils. She looked as innocently petrified as a doe. She turned her gaze to the floor and curled softly into her body. I froze and studied the scene as if it were a photograph. I hadn't touched her with a cruel hand or uttered an irate word and there she was, helpless, at my mercy. *My God*, I thought, *what power!*

Korama was numb to my presence when, at last, I sat down cross-legged next to her. Instead of hitting her as I had planned, I hugged her, picked the tape up off the floor, and placed it in her lap. My hands continued to shake, but not in anticipation. They were shaking because I had almost held an infant physically accountable for things she had no control over—my lethal choices in relationships, my poverty, my feelings of inadequacy; clearly, those were the circumstances at the root of my rage—and for what? Destroying a cassette tape that was worth no more than ten dollars? She was simply exploring and dissecting the world around her. She was trying to learn and, as her mother, it was my duty to teach and guide her, not punish her.

That incident prompted me to take a look at myself. Every relationship I had ever had was, in some way, abusive. In each one, I played the role of the victim. It was always the fault of someone else that I was not the person I wanted to be. From one involvement to the next, I carried blame, like a bouquet of flowers, and placed it in the open arms of my partner. It became clear to me that I opted to be with those people because they fulfilled my subconscious wishes to be mistreated; they re-created home for me. The fact that I was living out a dangerous cycle came without question. What I was unsure of was whether I would be able to break that cycle.

The highest vision I had of myself was far removed from the reality of my actions. I wanted desperately to be the mother I always dreamed of having when I was a child; I wanted to become the person I knew I was capable of being. For days afterward, I combed my brain, trying to figure out a way to change who I was. Then it dawned on me that I had already changed. The woman who approached her daughter in a crazed-frenzy was not the same one who sat next to her and offered maternal tenderness. Somewhere in the moment that separated those two women, I took responsibility for myself and for my emotions. I made a definitive choice to reject the patterns of my history.

Progress was slow. My financial troubles grew worse before they got better. And the anger, that righteous indignation which eased me into adulthood, did not automatically disappear. It lingered as depression for years but once I sought proper medical treatment, it too went away. However, during those first trying months, the bond I share with Korama found form and strengthened. Crucial compromises were made. For example, my books, cassettes, and other possessions that might be destroyed by a child's curiosity were placed on high shelves.

I shamefully admitted to myself that my inattentiveness to Korama in her earlier months was a passive type of abuse, but abuse nonetheless. Rather than continue to let her lie idly in her crib simply because she was not hungry or in need of a diaper change, I played with her and held conversations with her, as I had when she was in my womb. When Korama's first birthday came, it was as much a celebration for me as it was for her. In the twelve months it had taken her to learn how to walk, talk, trust, cultivate a solid personality, and use it to relate to others, I had relearned many of those very same things for myself.

Exactly three weeks and three days after Korama's birthday, the verdicts in the trial of the officers accused of using excessive force against Rodney King were announced. The largest civil insurrection in American history followed. From the safety of our Los Angeles home, Korama and I observed the violence through the windows and on television. It was harrowing. Everyone was using their anger as a justification to hurt someone else. As we watched, Korama stood beside me clutching my leg. I wondered how much of what was happening made any sense to her. Surely she was registering something. We think so little of what impact our actions have on children, especially those who are still nonverbal. What do we know or understand about how they process hurt, disillusionment? Korama had seen so much in her first year.

Violence breeds violence. That night I made a resolution in my heart to never strike Korama and to never invite abuse—of any sort—into our household. Keeping that resolution has been no simple feat. Korama, now five, is an intelligent child with a will as strong as stone. She is everything little girls arc not supposed to be: rough, aggressive, determined. She talks back—in several languages, using a patois of phrases pulled from English, Japanese, and Spanish, as well as Ga, my native tongue.

Needless to say, finding appropriate and effective methods of discipline that complement her development but do not involve physical force can be challenging. It requires patience, respect, and unwavering faith in the power of words. Admittedly, when I have been at my wits' end, the thought of spanking her has come to mind. It would be a quick fix, for the short run. But in spite of, or perhaps because of, my past, I recognize the importance of teaching Korama to understand that love and violence do not go together and should not be accepted when given hand-in-hand by the same person—be that person a lover, a friend, or a parent.

Several months ago, Korama and I were taking a trip together. A man seated next to us on the plane remarked, "What a cute little girl," then suddenly reached over to pat Korama on the head with one hand while pinching a chunk of her cheek with the other. Annoyed by the invasion of her space, Korama pulled back, looked him square in the eyes, and said firmly, "It's not nice for people to touch each other without asking. Please ask me next time." When I was her age, I didn't feel entitled to claim, let alone exhibit, such personal agency; I would have silently accepted the intrusion. That Korama did not made me proud. It was a sign that she—and I—were making great strides in our personal growth and that if we continued to travel the path we were on, both of us were going to turn out just fine.

Organizations to Contact

ACT for Kids
7 S. Howard, Suite 200, Spokane, WA 99201-3816
(509) 343-5020 • fax: (509) 747-0609
e-mail: resources@actforkids.org
Web site: www.actforkids.org

ACT for Kids is a nonprofit organization that provides resources to prevent and heal sexual abuse and other forms of family and social trauma. The organization also offers consultation, research, and training for the prevention and treatment of child abuse and sexual violence. ACT for Kids publications include workbooks, manuals, books, videos, and games.

Child Welfare Information Gateway
Children's Bureau/ACYF, Washington, DC 20024
(703) 385-7565
e-mail: info@childwelfare.gov (direct info)
Web site: www.childwelfare.gov

The Child Welfare Information Gateway recently consolidated services of the National Clearinghouse on Child Abuse and Neglect Information and the National Adoption Information Clearinghouse. The new organization provides access to print and electronic publications, Web sites, and online databases covering a wide range of topics, including child welfare, child abuse and neglect, adoption, search, and reunion. The organization offers various reports, fact sheets, and bulletins concerning child abuse and neglect.

Childhelp
15757 N. Seventy-eighth St., Scottsdale, Arizona 85260
(480) 922-8212 • fax: (480) 922-7061
Web site: www.childhelpusa.org

Childhelp is one of the oldest nonprofit organizations dedicated to the treatment, prevention, and research of child abuse and neglect. Childhelp's mission is to meet the physical, emotional, educational, and spiritual needs of abused and neglected children. The organization provides a broad range of programs that include residential treatment facilities, therapeutic group homes and foster homes, and child advocacy centers located across the United States.

FaithTrust Institute
2400 N. Forty-fifth St., #10, Seattle, WA   98103
(206) 634-1903 • fax: (206) 634-0115
e-mail: info@faithtrustinstitute.org.
Web site: www.faithtrustinstitute.org

FaithTrust Institute is an international, multifaith organization working to end sexual and domestic violence. FaithTrust offers a wide range of services and resources, including training, consultation, and educational materials, to provide communities and advocates with the tools and knowledge they need to address the religious and cultural issues related to abuse. In addition to information on the FaithTrust Web site, the organization sells videos, books, and educational materials.

The Family Violence Prevention Fund (FVPF)
383 Rhode Island St., Suite 304
San Francisco, CA   94103-5133
(415) 252-8900 • fax: (415) 252-8991
e-mail: info@endabuse.org
Web site: www.endabuse.org

FVPF works to prevent violence within the home and in the community. The organization was instrumental in developing the landmark Violence Against Women Act passed by Congress in 1994. FVPF has now expanded its reach to new audiences, including men and youth. The organization also assists health-care providers, police, judges, and employers in addressing family violence. FVPF offers a variety of fact sheets and personal stories of people, including celebrities, who have triumphed over family violence.

National Center on Elder Abuse (NCEA)
1201 Fifteenth St. NW, Suite 350
Washington, DC   20005-2482
(202) 898-2586 • fax: (202) 898-2583
e-mail: ncea@nasua.org
Web site: www.elderabusecenter.org

Funded by the U.S. Administration on Aging, NCEA offers resources on elder abuse, neglect, and exploitation. NCEA provides news and resources on elder rights; collaborates on research; provides consultation, education, and training; identifies and provides information about promising practices and interventions; and advises on policy development. The organization also offers statistics, surveys, and reading lists on various aspects of elder abuse.

National Coalition Against Domestic Violence (NCADV)
1120 Lincoln St., Suite 1603, Denver, CO   80203
(303) 839-1852 • fax: (303) 831-9251
e-mail: mainoffice@ncadv.org
Web site: www.ncadv.org

NCADV represents various state-run organizations that assist battered women and their children. NCADV works to eradicate social conditions that contribute to violence against women and children. NCADV also provides community-based services such as shelter programs and public education, and it lobbies for protective legislation. NCADV dispenses fact sheets that list local statistics and organizations for each state.

National Domestic Violence Hotline
3616 Far West Blvd., Suite 101-297, Austin, TX   78731-3074
(512) 453-8117
Web site: www.ndvh.org

The National Domestic Violence Hotline is available for counseling or referrals. The hotline offers an advocate who can talk about abusive situations, safety issues, and options for those threatened by violence in the home. All conversations with advocates at the National Hotline are strictly confidential.

National Network to End Domestic Violence (NNEDV)
660 Pennsylvania Ave. SE, Suite 303, Washington, DC   20003
(202) 543-5566 • fax: (202) 543-5626
Web site: www.nnedv.org

NNEDV lobbies for improved legislation to end family violence. The organization works to increase federal funding for
shelter programs and domestic violence coalitions and argues
for recognition of private and privileged communications for
survivors. Its sister organization, the National Network to End
Domestic Violence Fund (NNEDV Fund), provides more direct support to local programs and coalitions through public
awareness, outreach, funding, and training. The NNEDV Web
site provides updates on legislation and other general information.

Stop Abuse for Everyone (SAFE)
PO Box 951, Tualatin, OR   97062
e-mail: safe@safe4all.org
Web site: www.safe4all.org

SAFE is a human rights organization that provides services,
publications, and training to serve those who often get overlooked by domestic violence services: straight men, gays and
lesbians, teens, and the elderly. SAFE provides an online support group and resource lists for interested parties. It has
walk-in services in Illinois, New Hampshire, and Oregon.

The Rape, Abuse & Incest National Network (RAINN)
2000 L St. NW, Suite 406, Washington, DC   20036
(202) 544-1034 • fax: (202) 544-3556
e-mail: info@rainn.org
Web site: www.rainn.org

RAINN is America's largest antisexual-assault organization. In
addition to running the twenty-four-hour confidential national sexual assault hotline, RAINN provides information to
young people, student populations, and communities in general. The organization is a frequent resource for television, ra-
dio, and print news outlets on issues related to rape and sexual
assault.

For Further Research

Books

Lundy Bancroft, *When Dad Hurts Mom: Helping Your Children Heal the Wounds of Witnessing Abuse*. New York: Berkley, 2005.

Ellen Bass and Laura Davis, *Beginning to Heal: A First Book for Men and Women Who Were Sexually Abused as Children*. Rev. ed. New York: HarperCollins, 2003.

Marian Betancourt, *What to Do When Love Turns Violent: A Practical Resource for Women in Abusive Relationships*. New York: HarperPerennial, 1997.

Susan Brewster, *To Be an Anchor in the Storm: A Guide for Families and Friends of Abused Women*. Seattle: Seal, 2000.

Eve Buzama and Carl Buzama, *Domestic Violence: The Criminal Justice Response*. Thousand Oaks, CA: Sage, 2002.

Phillip W. Cook, *Abused Men: The Hidden Side of Domestic Violence*. Westport, CT: Praeger, 1997.

Barbara Cottrell, *When Teens Abuse Their Parents*. Halifax, Canada: Fernwood, 2005.

Dorothy Ayers Counts, Judith K. Brown, and Jacquelyn Campbell, eds., *To Have and to Hit: Cultural Perspectives on Wife Beating*. Champaign: University of Illinois Press, 1999.

Walter de Milly, *In My Father's Arms: A True Story of Incest*. Madison: University of Wisconsin Press, 2000.

Patricia Evans, *The Verbally Abusive Relationship: How to Recognize It and How to Respond*. Avon, MA: Adams Media, 1996.

Kate Havelin, *Child Abuse: Why Do My Parents Hit Me?* Mankato, MN: Capstone, 2000.

Judith Lewis Herman, *Trauma and Recovery: The Aftermath of Violence*. New York: Basic, 1992.

Ann Jones, *Next Time She'll Be Dead: Battering and How to Stop It*. Boston: Beacon, 2000.

Barrie Levy, *In Love and in Danger: A Teen's Guide to Breaking Free from Abusive Relationships*. Seattle: Seal, 1998.

Sandra E. Lundy and Beth Leventhal, eds., *Same-Sex Domestic Violence*. Thousand Oaks, CA: Sage, 1999.

Linda G. Mills, *Insult to Injury: Rethinking Our Responses to Intimate Abuse*. Princeton, NJ: Princeton University Press, 2003.

Jody Raphael, *Saving Bernice: Battered Women, Welfare and Poverty*. Boston: Northeastern University Press, 2000.

Beth Richie, *Compelled to Crime: The Gender Entrapment of Battered Black Women*. New York: Routledge, 1995.

Diane S. Sandell and Lois Hudson, *Ending Elder Abuse: A Family Guide*. Fort Bragg, CA: QED, 2000.

Dean Tong, *Elusive Innocence: Survival Guide for the Falsely Accused*. Lafayette, LA: Huntington House, 2001.

Susan Weitzman, *Not to People like Us: Hidden Abuse in Upscale Marriages*. New York: Basic, 2000.

Periodicals

Kimberly Barletto Becker and Laura Ann McCloskey, "Attention and Conduct Problems in Children Exposed to Family Violence," *American Journal of Orthopsychiatry*, 2002.

Tricia B. Bent-Goodley, "Perceptions of Domestic Violence: A Dialogue with African-American Women," *Health and Social Work*, November 2004.

Rosemary Chalk and Patricia King, "Facing Up to Family Violence," *Issues in Science and Technology*, Winter 1998–1999.

Lisa Collier Cool, "The Unspoken Pregnancy Danger: What Every Mother-to-Be Needs to Know About Domestic Violence," *Baby Talk*, December 1, 2003.

Wendy Davis, "Active Parenting: Sharwline Nicholson's Journey from Domestic Violence to Local Heroism," *City Limits*, June 2002.

David Fontes, "The Hidden Side of Domestic Violence: Male Victims," *Everyman*, June 30, 2000.

Greg Haller, "Domestic Violence: A Bottom-Line Issue: The Annual Pricetag Could Be as Much as $5 Billion," *Detroiter*, November December 2005.

Gerison Lansdown, "Children's Rights and Domestic Violence," *Child Abuse Review*, 2000.

Jennifer Leonard, "I Thought Everything Was My Fault," *Your Magazine*, August 2003.

Michel Marriott, "Angry Women, Battered Men: On the Other Side of Domestic Abuse, Sometimes It's the Brothers Who Get Hurt," *Essence*, November 2003.

Kim Ode, "The Other Side of Abuse; Men as Well as Women Need a Resource," *Minneapolis-St. Paul Star Tribune*, May 29, 2004.

Miriam Rozen, "The Good Fight," *Texas Lawyer*, September 26, 2005.

Susan Weitzman, "Painfully Privileged: Dr. Susan Weitzman Finds That Spousal Abuse Cuts Across All Economic Lines," *People Weekly*, July 2, 2001.

Kathy Young, "Abuse Revisited: A Feminist Challenges the Conventional Wisdom About Domestic Violence," *Reason*, April 2004.

Web Sites

National Center on Elder Abuse, "The 2004 Study of State Adult Protective Services: Abuse of Adults 60 Years of Age and Older February 2006." www.elderabusecenter. org.

Sam Vaknin, "How to Spot an Abuser on Your First Date," Women's Web, June 14, 2004. www.womensweb.ca.

Kathleen Waits, "Battered Women and Their Children: Lessons from One Woman's Story," *Houston Law Review*, 1998. www.houstonlawreview.org.

Index